George M. Fenn

The Star-Gazers

Volume 2

George M. Fenn

The Star-Gazers
Volume 2

ISBN/EAN: 9783337409654

Printed in Europe, USA, Canada, Australia, Japan

Cover: Foto ©Andreas Hilbeck / pixelio.de

More available books at **www.hansebooks.com**

BY

G. MANVILLE FENN

AUTHOR OF

'ELIS' CHILDREN,' 'A DOUBLE KNOT,' 'THE NEW MISTRESS,' ETC., ETC.

IN THREE VOLUMES

VOL. II.

Methuen & Co.

18 BURY STREET, W.C.

LONDON

1894

CONTENTS

—--o——

CHAPTER I.

CONTENTS.

THE STAR-GAZERS

THE STAR-GAZERS.

—o—

CHAPTER I.

AFTER A LAPSE.

IT was about a mile from the Alleynes' where the
sandy lane, going north, led by an eminence, rugged,
scarped, and crowned with great columnar firs that
must have sprung from seeds a couple of hundred
years ago. By day, when the sun shone in from the
east at his rising, or from the west at his going down,
the great towering trunks that ran up seventy or
eighty feet without a branch looked as if cast in ruddy
bronze, while overhead the thick, dark, boughs inter-
laced and shut out the sky.

It was a gloomy enough spot by day amidst the
maze of tall columns, with the ground beneath
slippery from the dense carpeting of pine needles;
by night, whether a soft breeze was overhead whispering in imitation of the surging waves, or it was a
storm, there was ever that never-ending sound of the

sea upon the shore, making the place in keeping with
the spirit of him who sought for change and relief
from troublous thoughts.

Moray Alleyne's brain was full of trouble, of
imperious thoughts that would not be kept back,
and one night, to calm his disturbed spirit, he went
out from the observatory, bare-headed, to walk for a
few minutes up and down the garden.

But there was no rest there, and, feeling confined
and cribbed within fence and hedge, he glanced for a
moment or two at the tall window with its undrawn
blinds, through which he could see Mrs Alleyne,
seated stiff and with an uncompromising look upon
her face, busy stitching at a piece of linen in which
she was making rows of the finest nature, in preparation for a garment to be worn by her son.

Lucy was at the other side of the table, also
working, but, as the lamplight fell upon her face,
Alleyne could see that it was unruffled and full of
content.

He sighed as he turned away, and thought of the
past, when his thoughts went solely to his absorbing
work—when this strange attraction, as he termed it,
had not come upon him and drawn him, as it were,
out of his course.

Only a short time back, and he went on in his
matter-of-fact, mundane orbit, slowly working out
problems, sometimes failing, but always returning to
the task with the same calm peaceful serenity of

spirit, waiting patiently for the triumph of science
that sooner or later came for his reward.

How calm and unruffled all this had been. No
fever of the soul, no tempest of spirit to disturb the
even surface of his life. But now all was changed.
They had torn him amongst them from the happy,
placid life, to give him rage, and bitterness and
pain.

His brow grew rugged and his hands clenched as
he walked rapidly out on to the wild heath, heedless
of the bushes and the inequalities of the ground, until
he fell heavily, and leaped up again, to turn back.
Then, giving up the wide waste of moor which he had
instinctively chosen as being in accord with his frame
of mind, he made straight for the next desolate spot,
where it seemed to him that he could be alone with
his thoughts, and perhaps school them into subjec-
tion.

'Cool down this madness,' he once said aloud,
laughing bitterly the while; and the sound of his
strange voice made him start and hurry on along the
shady lane, as if to escape from the unseen monitor
who had reminded him of his suffering.

' Yes, it is madness,' he muttered, ' I could not have
believed it true. But, discipline, patience, I shall
conquer yet.'

He walked on, with the beads of perspiration
coming softly out upon his brow ; then, from being
like a fine dew, they began to join one with the other,

till they stood out in great drops unheeded, as he went swiftly on, and almost blindly at last turned rapidly up the steep ascent, climbing at times, and avoiding the pine trunks by a kind of blind instinct. He toiled on farther and farther, till he stood at the highest part of the great natural temple, with its wind-swept roof hidden in the darkness overhead, and two huge pines bending over to each other, like the sides of some huge east window, at the precipitous broken edge of the hill.   Through this he could look straight away over the intervening billowy estate, to where Brackley Hall stood surrounded by trees, and with its lights shining softly against a vast background of darkness.

And now as he rested a hand upon a trunk, his vivid imagination pictured Glynne as being there, behind one or other of the softly-illumined panes.

Here he stopped and stood motionless for a time, gazing straight before him through the dimly-seen vista of the trunks, breathing in the soft, cool night air, dry and invigorating at that height.   All was so still and silent, that, obeying his blind instinct, he seemed to have come there to find calmness and repose.

But they were not present ; neither was the place dark—to him.   For, as he stood there, with knotted brow, and teeth and hands clenched, turn which way he would there was light, and within that light, gazing at him with its intense, rapt expression—as if living and breathing upon his words—the one face that always haunted him now.

It had been so strange at first—that look of thoughtful veneration, that air of belief. Then, from being half-pleased, half-flattered, had come the time when it had created a want in his life—the desire to be master and go on teaching this obedient disciple who dwelt upon his words, took them so faithfully to heart, and waited patiently for fresh utterances from his lips.

It was not love on her part. He knew that. He was sure of it. At least it was the love of the science that he strove to teach—the thirsting of a spirit to know more and more of the wonders of infinite space. She liked to be in his society, to listen to his words. He knew he was gauging Glynne Day's heart, when, with a sensation of misery that swept over him like some icy wave, he went over the hours they had spent together. But, when he tried to gauge his own he trembled, and asked himself why this madness had come upon him, robbing him of his peace and rest—making him so unfit for his daily work.

He strode on to and fro, winding in and out amongst the tall pillars of this darkened nature-temple, fighting his mental fight and praying from time to time for help to crush down the madness that had assailed him where he had thought himself so strong.

Strive how he would, though, there was Glynne's

face ever gazing up into his; and beside it, half-mockingly, in its calm, satisfied content, was Rolph's; and as he met the eyes, there was the cool, contemptuous, pitying look, such as he had seen upon the young officer's face again and again, mingled with the arrogant air of dislike that he made so little effort to conceal.

For a time Alleyne had been growing calmer; his determined efforts to master himself had seemed as if about to be attended with success; but as in fancy he had seen Rolph's face beside that of Glynne, a feeling of rage—of envious rage—that mastered him in turn held sway.

But it was not for long; the power of a well-disciplined brain was brought to bear, and Moray Alleyne stood at last with his arms folded, leaning against a tree, thinking that after this mad ebullition of passion, he had gained the victory, and that henceforth all this was going to be as a bygone dream.

It must have been by some occult law of attraction that deals with human beings as inanimate objects are drawn together upon the surface of a pond, that Rolph, in contemptuous scorn of the sedative tea that would be on the way in Sir John's drawing-room, and holding himself free for a little self-indulgence, took three cigars from his future father-in-law's cabinet in the smoking-room, secured a box of matches, and, after putting on a light overcoat and soft hat, strolled out on to the lawn.

'Been on duty with her all day,' he said, with a half laugh, 'and a fellow can't quite give himself up to petticoat government—not hers. If it wasn't for Aldershot being so near, it would be awful.'

Glynne was seated alone in the drawing-room, where the shaded lamp stood on the side-table, deep in a book that she was reading with avidity ; and as Rolph, with his hands in his pockets, strolled round the house, he, too, stopped to look in at the window.

'There's no nonsense about it,' he said, 'she is pretty—I might say beautiful, and there isn't a girl in the regiment who comes near her.'

'Humph! what a chance. The old boys are snoring in the dining-room, each with a handkerchief over his head, and for the next two hours I dare say we should be alone, and—drink tea!' he said with an air of disgust. 'I hope she won't be so confoundedly fond of tea when we're married. It's rather too much of a good thing sometimes. And a man wants change.'

He thrust his hands deeply into his coat pockets, where one of them came in contact with a cigar, which he took out, bit off the end mechanically, and stood rolling it to and fro between his lips.

'Shall I go in?' he asked himself. 'Hang it, no! If one's too much with a girl she'll grow tired of you before marriage. Better keep her off a little, and not spoil her too soon. Yes, she really is a very handsome girl. Just fancy her in one of the smartest dresses a tip-top place could turn out, and sitting beside a fellow on a four-in-hand—Ascot, say, or to some big meet. There won't be many who will put us—her, I mean '—he added, with a dash of modesty—' in the shade. Here, I'll go and have a talk to her. No, I won't. I sha'n't get my cigar if I do. We shall have plenty of *tête-à-têtes*, I dare say. And I promised to-night— What's she reading, I wonder? Last new novel, I suppose. Puzzles me,' he said to himself, as he swung round ' how a woman can go on reading novels at the rate some of them do. Such stuff! It's only about one in a hundred that is written by anybody who knows what life really is— about horses and dogs—and sport,' he added after a little thought. 'Poor little Glynne. It pleases her, though, and I sha'n't interfere, but she might cultivate subjects more that agree with my tastes—say the hunt—and the field.'

He gave one glance over his shoulder at the picture of the reading girl in the drawing-room and then went off across the lawn, to be stopped by the wire fence, against which he paused as if measuring its height. Then going back for a dozen yards or so he took a sharp run, meaning to leap it, but stopped short close to the wire.

' Won't do,' he muttered ; ' too dark.'

He then stepped over it, bending the top wire down and making it give a loud twang when released, as he walked on sharply towards the footway that crossed the path and led away to the fir woods, whistling the while.

Perhaps if he had known that the book Glynne was reading with such eagerness did not happen to be a novel, but a study of the heavens, by one, Mr Lockyer, the ideas that coursed through his mind would not have been of quite so complacent a character—that is to say, if the strain upon his nature to supply him with muscles and endurance had left him wit enough to put that and that together, and judge by the result.

'It's getting precious dull here, and home's horrid,' said Rolph, as he stopped in the shadow of a tree, whose huge trunk offered shelter from the breeze.

Here he proceeded, in the quiet deliberate fashion of a man who makes a study of such matters, and who would not on any consideration let a cigar burn sidewise, to light the roll he held in his teeth. He struck a match, coquetted with the flame, holding it near and drawing it away, till the leaf was well alight, when he placed his hands in his pockets, and walked on, puffing complacently, for a short distance at a moderate pace, but, finding the path easy and smooth, his mind began to turn to athletics, and, taking his hands from his pockets, he stopped short and doubled his fists.

'Won't do to get out of condition with this domestic spaniel life,' he said, with a laugh, and, drawing a long breath, he set off walking, taking long, regular strides, and getting over the ground at a tremendous pace for about half a mile, when he stopped short to smile complacently.

'Not bad that,' he said aloud, 'put out my cigar though;' and, again sheltering himself behind a tree, he struck a match and relit the roll of tobacco.

'I must do a little more of this early of a morning,' he said, as he regained his breath, and cooled down gradually by slowly walking on, and as fate arranged it, entering the great fir clump on the side farthest from the lane.

'They say the smell of the fir is healthy, and does a man good,' said Rolph. 'I'll have a good sniff or two.'

There was more of the odour of tobacco, though, than of the pines, as with his footsteps deadened by the soft, half-decayed vegetable matter, he threaded his way amongst the tall trunks.

'Humph! moon rising! see the gates!' said Rolph, with a satisfied air, as if the great yellow orb, slowly rising above the wood and darting horizontal rays through the pines, were illumining the path for his special benefit. Then he looked at his watch. 'Ten minutes too soon. But I dare say she's waiting. If this place were mine I should have all these trees cut down for timber and firewood. Fetch a lot!'

The wondrous effects of black velvety darkness and golden lines of light were thrown away upon the young baronet, who saw in the pale gilding of the tree trunks only so much to avoid.

All at once his thoughts took a turn in another direction, and unwittingly he began to ponder upon the intimacy that had grown up between the people at the Hall and the Alleynes.

'It's a great mistake, and I don't like it,' Rolph said to himself. 'That fellow hangs about after Glynne like some great dog. I shall have to speak to the old man about it. Glynne doesn't see it, of course, and I don't mean that she should, but it gets to be confoundedly unpleasant to a—to a thoughtful man—to a man of the world. Wiser, perhaps, to have a few words with the fellow himself, and tell him what I think of his conduct. I will too,' he said, after a pause. 'He is simply ignorant of the common decencies of society, or he wouldn't do it. I shall— What the devil's he doing here—come to watch?'

Rolph stopped short, completely astounded upon seeing, not two yards away, the statue-like figure of Alleyne, with arms folded, leaning against a tree, thoroughly intent upon his thoughts.

For some time neither Rolph nor Alleyne spoke, the latter being profoundly ignorant of the presence of the former.

The shadows of the fir wood, as well as those of Alleyne's mind, were to blame for this, for where Rolph had paused the moonbeams had not touched, and though Alleyne's eyes were turned in that direction, they were filmed by the black darkness of the future, a deep shadow that he could not pierce. But by degrees, as the great golden shield, whose every light or speck was as familiar to him as his daily life, swept slowly on, a broad bar of darkness passed to his left, revealing first a part, then the whole of Sir Robert Rolph's figure, as he stood scowling there, his hands in his pockets, and puff after puff of smoke coming from his lips.

Some few moments glided by before Alleyne realised the truth. He had been thinking so deeply —so bitterly of his rival, that it seemed as if his imagination had evoked this figure, and that his nerves had been so overstrained that this was some waking dream.

Then came the reaction, making him start violently, as Rolph emitted a tremendous cloud of smoke, and then said shortly, without taking his cigar from his lips,—

'How do?'

'Captain Rolph!' cried Alleyne, finding speech at last.

'That's me. Well, what is it?'

There was another pause, for what appeared to be an interminable time. Alleyne wished to speak, but his lips were sealed. Years of quiet, thoughtful life had made him, save when led on by some object in which he took deep interest, slow of speech, while now the dislike, more than the disgust this man caused him, seemed to have robbed him of all power of reply.

'Confounded cad!' thought Rolph; 'he is watching;' and then, aloud, 'Star-gazing and mooning?'

The bitterly contemptuous tone in which this was said stung Alleyne to the quick, and he replied, promptly,—

'No.'

There was something in that tone that startled Rolph for the moment, but he was of too blunt and heavy a nature to detect the subtle meaning a tone of voice might convey, and, seizing the opportunity that had come to him, he ran at it with the clumsiness of a bull at some object that offends its eye.

'Hang the cad, there couldn't be a better chance,' he said to himself; and, adopting the attitude popular with cavalry officers not largely addicted to brains, he straddled as if on horseback, and setting his feet down as though he expected each heel to make the rowel of a spur to ring, he walked straight up to Alleyne, smoking furiously, and puffed a cloud almost into his face.

'Look here, Mr—Mr—er—Alleyne,' he said, loudly, 'I wanted to talk to you, and present time seems as suitable as any other time.'

Alleyne had recovered himself, and bowed coldly.

'I was not aware that Captain Rolph had any communication to make to me,' he said quietly.

'S'pose not,' replied Rolph, offensively; 'people of your class never do.—Hang the cad! He is spying so as to get a pull on me,' he muttered to himself.

'I'm just in the humour, and for two pins I'd give him as good a thrashing as I really could.'

'Will you proceed,' said Alleyne, in whose pale cheeks a couple of spots were coming, for it was impossible not to read the meaning of the other's words and tone.

'When I please,' said Rolph, in the tone of voice he would have adopted towards some groom, or to one of the privates of his troop.

Alleyne bowed his head and stood waiting, for he said to himself—'I am in the wrong—I am bitterly to blame. Whatever he says, I will bear without a word.'

A deep silence followed, for, though Rolph pleased to speak, he could not quite make up his mind what to say. He did not wish to blurt out anything, he told himself, that should compromise his dignity, nor yet to let Alleyne off too easily. Hence, being unprepared, he was puzzled.

'Look here, you know,' he said at last, and angrily; for he was enraged with himself for his want of words, 'you come a good deal to Sir John's.'

'Yes, I am invited,' said Alleyne, quietly.

Rolph's rehearsal was gone.

'I'll let him have it,' he muttered ; 'I'm not going to fence and spar. Yes,' he cried aloud, 'I know you are. Sir John's foolishly liberal in that way ; but you know, Mr Allen, or Alleyne, or whatever your name is, I'm not blind.'

Alleyne remained silent ; and, being now wound up, Rolph swaggered and straddled about with an imaginary horse between his legs.

' Look here, you know, I don't want to be hard on a man who is ready to own that he is in the wrong, and apologises, and keeps out of the way for the future ; but this sort of thing won't do. By Jove, no, it sha'n't do, you know. I won't have it. Do you hear ? I won't have it.'

Something seemed to rise to Moray Alleyne's throat—some vital force to run through his nerves and muscles, making them twitch and quiver, as the young officer went on in an increasingly bullying tone. For some moments Alleyne, of the calm, peaceful existence, did not realise what it meant— what this sensation was ; but at last it forced itself upon him that it was the madness of anger, the fierce desire of a furious man to seize an enemy and struggle with him till he is beaten down, crushed beneath the feet.

As he realised all this he wondered and shrank within himself, gazing straight before him with knitted brows and half-closed eyes.

' You see,' continued Rolph, ' I always have my eyes open—make a point of keeping my eyes open, and it's time you understood that, because Miss—'

' Silence !' cried Alleyne fiercely.

' What! What do you mean ?' cried Rolph, as if he was addressing some delinquent in his regiment.

'Confound it all! How dare you, sir! How dare you speak to me like that?'

'Say what you like, speak what you will to me,' said Alleyne, excitedly, 'but let that name be held sacred. It must not be drawn into this quarrel.'

'How dare you, sir! How dare you!' roared Rolph. 'What do you mean in dictating to me what I should say? Name held sacred? Drawn into this —what do you say—quarrel. Do you think I should stoop to quarrel with you?'

Alleyne raised one hand deprecatingly.

'I'd have you to know, sir, that I am telling you that I am not blind,'—he repeated this as if to mend his observations—'I tell you to keep away from the Hall, and to recollect that because a certain lady has condescended to speak to you in the innocency of her heart—yes, innocency of her heart,' he repeated, for it was a phrase that pleased him, and sounded well—'it is not for you to dare to presume to talk to her as you do—to look at her as you do—or to come to the Hall as you do. I've watched you, and I've seen your looks and ways—confound your insolence! And now, look here, if ever you dare to presume to speak to Miss—to the lady, I mean, as you have addressed her before, I'll take you, sir, and horse-whip you till you cannot stand. Do you hear, sir; do you hear? Till you cannot stand.'

Alleyne stood there without speaking, while this brutal tirade was going on. His breast heaved, and his breath was drawn heavily; but he gave no sign, and presuming upon the success that had attended his speaking, Rolph continued with all the offensiveness of tone and manner that he had acquired from his colonel, a rough, overbearing martinet of the old school.

'I cannot understand your presumption,' continued Rolph. 'I cannot understand of what you have been thinking, coming cringing over to the Hall, day after day, forcing your contemptible twaddle about stars and comets, and such far-fetched nonsense upon unwilling ears. Good heavens, sir! are you mad, or a fool?—I say, do you hear me—what are you, mad or a fool?'

Still Alleyne did not reply, but listened to his rival's words with so bitter a feeling of anguish at his heart, that it took all his self-command to keep him from groaning aloud.

And still Rolph went on, for, naturally sluggish of mind, it took some time to bring that mind, as he would have termed it, into action. Once started, however, he found abundance of words of a sort, and he kept on loudly, evidently pleased with what he was saying, till once more he completed the circle in which he had been galloping, and ended with,—

'You hear me—thrash you as I would a dog.'

Rolph had run down, and, coughing to clear away the huskiness of his throat, he muttered to himself,—

'Cigar's out.'

Hastily taking another from his pocket, he bit off the end, lit up, gave a few puffs, scowling at Alleyne the while, and then said loudly,—

'And now you understand, I think, sir?'

There were spurs imaginary jingling at Rolph's heels, and the steel scabbard of a sabre banging about his legs, as he turned and strode away, whistling.

And then there was silence amidst the tall columnar pines, which looked as if carved out of black marble, save where the moonlight streamed through, cutting them sharply as it were, leaving some with bright patches of light, and dividing others into sections of light and darkness. There was not even a sigh now in the dark branches overhead, not a sound but the heavy, hoarse breathing of Moray Alleyne, as he stood there fighting against the terrible emotion that made him quiver.

He had listened to the coarsely brutal language of this man of athleticism, borne his taunts, his insults, as beneath him to notice, for there was another and a greater mental pain whose contemplation seemed to madden him till his sufferings were greater than he could bear.

If it had been some bright, talented man—officer, civilian, cleric, anything, so that he had been worthy and great, he could have borne it; but for Glynne, whose sweet eyes seemed day by day to be growing fuller of wisdom, whose animated countenance was

brightening over with a keener intelligence that told
of the workings of a mind whose latent powers
were beginning to dawn, to be pledged to this overbearing brutal man of thews and sinews, it was a
sacrilege ; and, after standing there, forgetful of his
own wrongs, the insults that he had borne unmoved,
he suddenly seemed to awaken to his agony ; and,
uttering a bitter cry, he flung himself face downwards
upon the earth.

'Glynne, my darling—my own love !'

There was none to hear, none to heed, as he lay
there clutching at the soft loose pine needles for a
time, and then lying motionless, lost to everything—
to time, to all but his own misery and despair.

CHAPTER II.

ATTRACTION.

A FEW moments later there was a faint rustling noise as of some one hurrying over the fir needles, and a lightly-cloaked figure came for an instant into the moonlight, but shrank back in among the tree-trunks.

'Rob!' was whispered—'Rob, are you there?'

Alleyne started up on one elbow, and listened as the voice continued,—

'Don't play with me, dear. I couldn't help being late. Father seemed as if he would never go out.'

There was a faint murmur among the heads of the pines, and the voice resumed.

'Rob, dear, don't—pray don't. I'm so nervous and frightened. Father might be watching me. I know you're there, for I heard you whistle.'

Alleyne remained motionless. He wanted to speak but no words came ; and he waited as the new comer seemed to be listening till a faintly-heard whistling of an air came on the still night air from somewhere below in the sandy lane.

'Ah!' came from out of the darkness, sounding like an eager cry of joy ; and she who uttered the cry darted off with all the quickness of one accustomed to the woods, taking almost instinctively the road pursued by Rolph, and overtaking him at the end of a few minutes.

'Rob—Rob!' she panted.

'Hush, stupid!' he growled. 'You've come then at last. See any one among the trees ?'

'No, dear, not a soul. Oh, Rob, I thought I should never be able to come to-night.'

'Humph! Didn't want to, I suppose.'

'Rob!'

Only one word, but the tone of reproach sounded piteous.

'Why weren't you waiting, then ?—You were not up yonder, were you ?' he added sharply.

'No, dear. I've only just got here. Father seemed as if he would never go out to-night, and it is a very, very long way to come.'

'Hullo! How your heart beats. Why, Judy, you must go into training. You are out of condition. I can feel it thump.'

'Don't, Rob, pray. I want to talk to you. It's dreadfully serious.'

'Then I don't want to hear it.'

'But you must, dear. Remember all you've said. Listen to me, pray.'

'Well, go on. What is it ?'

'Rob, dear, I'm in misery—in agony always. You're staying again at Brackley, and after all you said.'

'Man can't do as he likes, stupid little goose; not in society. I must break it off gently.'

There was a low moan out of the darkness where the two figures stood, and, added to the mysterious aspect of the lane where all was black below, but silvered above by the moonbeams.

'What a sigh,' whispered Rolph.

'Rob, dear, pray. Be serious now. I want you to listen. You must break all that off.'

'Of course. It's breaking itself off. Society flirtation, little goose; and if you'll only be good, all will come right.'

'Oh, Rob, if you only knew!'

'Well, it was your fault. If you hadn't been so cold and stand-offish, I shouldn't have gone and proposed to her. Now, it must have time.'

'You're deceiving me, dear; and it is cruel to one who makes every sacrifice for your sake.'

'Are you going to preach like this for long? Because if so, I'm off.'

'Rob!' in a piteous tone. 'I've no one to turn to but you, and I'm in such trouble. What can I do if you forsake me. I came to-night because I want your help and counsel.'

'Well, what is it?'

'Father would kill me if he knew I'd come.'

'Ben Hayle's a fool. I thought he was fond of you.'

'He is, dear. He worships me; but you've made me love you, Rob, and though I want to obey him I can't forget you. I can't keep away.'

'Of course you can't. It's nature, little one.'

'Rob, will you listen to me?'

'Yes. Be sharp then.'

'Pray break that off then at once at Brackley, and come to father and ask him to let us be married directly.'

'No hurry.'

'No hurry?—If you knew what I'm suffering.'

'There, there; don't worry, little one. It's all right, I tell you. Do you think I'm such a brute as to throw you over? See how I chucked Madge for your sake.'

'Yes, dear, yes; I do believe in you,' came with a sob, 'in spite of all; and I have tried, and will try so hard, Rob, to make myself a lady worthy of you. I'd do anything sooner than you should be ashamed of me. But, Rob, dear—father—'

'Hang father!'

'Don't trifle, dear. You can't imagine what I have suffered, and what he suffers. All those two long weary months since we left the lodge it has been dreadful. He keeps on advertising and trying, but no one will engage him. It is as if some one always whispered to gentlemen that he was once a poacher, and it makes him mad.'

'Well, I couldn't help my mother turning him off.'

'Couldn't help it, dear! Oh, Rob!'

'There you go again. Now, come, be sensible. I must get back soon.'

'To her!' cried Judith, wildly.

'Nonsense. Don't be silly. She's like a cold fish to me. It will all come right.'

'Yes, if you will come and speak to my father.'

'Can't.'

'Rob, dear,' cried Judith in a sharp whisper; 'you must, or it will be father's ruin. He has begun to utter threats.'

'Threats? He'd better not.

'It's in his despair, dear. He says it's your fault if he, in spite of his trying to be honest, is driven back to poaching.'

He'd better take to it! Bah! Let him threaten. He knows better. Nice prospect for me to marry a poacher's daughter.'

'Oh, Rob, how can you be so cruel. You don't know.'

'Know what? Does he threaten anything else?'

'Yes,' came with a suppressed sob.

'What?'

'I dare not tell you. Yes, I must. I came on purpose to-night. Just when I felt that I would stay by him and not break his heart by doing what he does not want.'

'Talk sense, silly. People's hearts don't break. Only horses', if you ride them too hard.'

Judith uttered a low sob.

'Well, what does he say?'

'That you are the cause of all his trouble, and that you shall make amends, or—'

'Or what?'

'I dare not tell you,' sobbed the girl, passionately. 'But, Rob, you will have pity on him—on me, dear, and make him happy again.'

'Look here,' said Rolph, roughly. 'Ben Hayle had better mind what he is about. Men have been sent out of the country for less than that, or—well, something of the kind. I'm not the man to be bullied by my mother's keeper, so let's have no more of that. Now, that's enough for one meeting. You wrote to Aldershot for me to meet you, and the letter was sent to me at Brackley, of course. So I came expecting to find you pretty and loving, instead of which your head's full of cock-and-bull nonsense, and you're either finding fault or telling me about your father's bullying. Let him bully. I shall keep my promise to you when I find it convenient. Nice tramp for me to come at this time of night.'

'It's a long walk from Lindham here in the dark, Rob, dear,' said the girl.

'Oh, yes, but you've nothing to do. There, I'll think about Ben Hayle and his getting a place, but I don't want you to be far away, Judy.—Now, don't be

absurd.—What are you struggling about?—Hang the
girl, it's like trying to hold a deer. Judy! You're not
gone. Come here. I can see you by that tree.'

There was a distant rustling, and Captain Rolph
uttered an oath.

'Why, she has gone!'

It was quite true. Judith was running fast in the
direction of the cottages miles away in the wild
common land of Lindham, and Rolph turned upon
his heel and strode back toward Brackley.

'Time I had one of the old man's brandy-and-
sodas,' he growled. 'Better have stopped and talked
to my saint. Ben Hayle going back to poaching!
Threaten me with mischief if I don't marry her! I
wish he would take to it again.'

Rolph walked on faster, getting excited by his
thoughts, and, after hurrying along for a few hundred
yards, he said aloud,—

'And get caught.'

'Now for a run,' he added, a minute later. 'This
has been a pleasant evening and no mistake. Ah,
well, all comes right in the end.'

CHAPTER III.

A SEARCH.

ABOUT a couple of hours earlier there was a ring at the gaunt-looking gate at the Firs, and that ring caused Mrs Alleyne's Eliza to start as if galvanised, and to draw her feet sharply over the sanded floor, and beneath her chair.

Otherwise Eliza did not move. She had been darning black stockings, and as her feet went under her chair, she sat there with the light—a yellow and dim tallow dip, set up in a great tin candlestick—staring before her, lips and eyes wide open, one hand and arm covered with a black worsted stocking, the fingers belonging to the other arm holding up a stocking needle, motionless, as if she were so much stone.

Anon, the bell, which hid in a little pent-house of its own high up on the ivied wall, jangled again, and a shock of terror ran through Eliza's body once more, but only for her to relapse into the former cataleptic state.

Then came a third brazen clanging; and this time the kitchen door opened, and Eliza uttered a squeal.

'Why, Eliza,' cried Lucy, 'were you asleep? The

gate bell has rung three times. Go and see who
it is.'

'Oh, please, miss, I dursn't,' said Eliza with a shiver.

'Oh, how can you be so foolish!' cried Lucy.
'There, bring the light, and I'll come with you.'

'There—there was a poor girl murdered once,
miss,' stammered Eliza, 'at a gate. Please, miss, I
dursn't go.'

'Then I must go myself,' cried Lucy. 'Don't be
so silly. Mamma will be dreadfully cross if you
don't come.'

Eliza seemed to think that it would be better to
risk being murdered at the gate than encounter Mrs
Alleyne's anger, so she started up, caught at the tin
candlestick with trembling hand, and then unbolted
the kitchen door loudly, just as the bell was about to
be pulled for the fourth time.

'You speak, please, miss,' whispered the girl. 'I
dursn't. Pray say something before you open the
gate.'

'Who's there,' cried Lucy.

'Only me, Miss Alleyne,' said a well-known voice.
'I was coming across the common, and thought I'd
call and see how your brother is.'

Lucy eagerly began to unfasten the great gate, but
for some reason, probably best known to herself, she
stopped suddenly, coloured a little, and said—almost
sharply,—

'Quick, Eliza, why don't you open the gate?'

Thus adjured, the maiden unfastened the ponderous lock, and admitted Philip Oldroyd, who shook hands warmly with Lucy, and then seemed as if he were about to change her hand over to his left, and feel her pulse with his right.

'We always have the gate locked at dusk,' said Lucy, 'the place stands so lonely, and—'

'You feel a little nervous,' said Oldroyd, smiling, as they walked up to the house.

'Oh, no!' said Lucy, eagerly; 'I never think there is anything to mind, but the maid is terribly alarmed lest we should be attacked by night. My brother is out,' she hastened to say, to fill up a rather awkward pause. 'He is taking one of your prescriptions,' she added, archly.

'Wise man,' cried Oldroyd, as they passed round to the front door and went in. 'I suppose he will not be long?'

'Oh, no!' said Lucy, eagerly; 'if you will come in and wait, he is sure to be back soon.'

Then she hesitated, and hastened to speak again, feeling quite uncomfortable and guilty, as if she had been saying something unmaidenly—as if she had been displaying an eagerness for the young doctor to stop—when all the time she told herself, it was perfectly immaterial, and she did not care in the least.

'Of course I can't be sure,' she added, growing a little quicker of speech; 'but I think he will not be long. He has gone round by the pine wood.'

'Then I should meet him if I went that way,' said Oldroyd, who had also become rather awkward and hesitant.

'Oh, yes; I think you would be sure to meet him,' cried Lucy eagerly.

'Thanks,' said Oldroyd, who felt rather vexed that she should be eager to get rid of him; 'then perhaps I had better go.'

'But of course I can't tell which way he will come back,' cried Lucy, hastily; 'and you might miss him.'

'To be sure, yes,' said Oldroyd, taking heart again; 'so I might, and then not see him at all.' And he looked anxiously at Lucy's troubled face over the tin candlestick, ornamented with drops of tallow that had fallen upon its sides, while Eliza slowly closed the front door, and gazed with her lips apart from one to the other.

Lucy was all repentance again, for in a flash her conscience had told her that she had seemed eager, and pressed the doctor to stay.

An awkward pause ensued, one which neither the visitor nor Lucy seemed able to break. Each tried very hard to find something to say, but in vain.

'How stupid of me!' thought Lucy, angrily.

'What's come to me?' thought Oldroyd; the only idea beside being that he ought to ask Lucy about her health, only he could not, for it would seem so professional. So he looked helplessly at her, and she returned his look half indignantly, while the candle was held on one side, and Eliza gaped at them wonderingly.

Mrs Alleyne ended the awkward pause by opening the dining-room door, and standing there framed like a silhouette.

'Oh, is it you, Mr Oldroyd?' she said, quietly.

'Yes, good evening,' exclaimed the young doctor, quickly, like one released from a spell; 'as I told Miss Alleyne here, I was coming close by, and I thought I would call and see how Mr Alleyne is.'

'We are very glad to see you,' said Mrs Alleyne, with grave courtesy. 'Pray come in, Mr Oldroyd,' and Lucy uttered a low sigh of satisfaction.

'Of course this is not a professional visit, Mrs Alleyne,' said Oldroyd; and then he wished he had not said it, for Mrs Alleyne's face showed the lines a little more deeply, and there was a slight twitching about her lips.

'I am sorry that Mr Alleyne has not yet returned,' she said, and as soon as they were seated, she smiled, and tried to remove the restraint that had fallen upon them in the dreary room.

'I am very grateful to you, Mr Oldroyd,' she said; my son is wonderfully better.'

'And would be in a position to laugh all doctors in the face, if he would carry out my prescriptions a little more fully,' said Oldroyd. 'But we must not be too hard upon him. I think it is a great thing to wean him from his studies as we have.'

'You dreadfully conceited man,' thought Lucy. 'How dare you have the shamelessness to think you have done all this! I know better. No man could have done it—there.'

'Did you speak, Miss Alleyne?' said Oldroyd, looking round suddenly, and finding Lucy's eyes intent upon him.

'I? No,' cried Lucy, flushing ; and then biting her lips with annoyance, because her cheeks burned, 'I was listening to you and mamma.'

'It is quite time Moray returned,' said Mrs Alleyne, anxiously glancing towards the closed window.

'Yes, mamma ; we shall hear his step directly,' said Lucy.

'He does not generally stay so long,' continued Mrs Alleyne, going to the window to draw aside the curtain and look out. 'Did he say which way he would go, Lucy?'

'Yes, mamma. I asked him, and he said as far as the fir wood.'

'Ah, yes,' responded Mrs Alleyne ; 'he says he can think so much more easily among the great trees— that his mind seems able to plunge into the depths of the vast abysses of the heavens.'

'I don't believe he does think about stars at all,' thought Lucy. 'I believe he goes there to stare across the park, and think about Glynne.'

A feeling of elation made the girl's heart glow, and her eyes sparkle, as she more and more began to nurse this, one of the greatest ideas of her heart. It was an exceedingly immoral proceeding on her part, for she knew that Glynne was engaged to be married to Captain Rolph; but him she utterly detested, she told herself, and that it was an entire mistake; in fact, she assured herself that it would be an act of the greatest benevolence, and one for which she would receive the thanks of both parties all through her lifetime—if she could succeed in breaking off the engagement and marrying Glynne to her brother.

The conversation went on, but it was checked from time to time by Mrs Alleyne again rising to go to the window, and this movement on her part always had the effect of making Lucy's eyes drop immediately upon her work; and, though she had been the minute before frankly meeting Oldroyd's gaze in conversation, such remarks as he addressed to her now were answered with her look averted, as she busied herself over her sewing.

'Moray never stayed so late as this before,' said Mrs Alleyne, suddenly, turning her pale face on those who were so wrapped in their own thoughts that they had almost forgotten the absentee.

'No, mamma,' cried Lucy, reproaching herself for her want of interest; 'he is an hour later.'

'It is getting on towards two hours beyond his

time,' cried Mrs Alleyne, in despairing tones. 'I am very uneasy.'

'Oh, but he has only gone a little farther than usual, mamma, dear,' cried Lucy; 'pray don't be uneasy.'

'I cannot help it, my child,' cried Mrs Alleyne; 'he who is so punctual in all his habits would never stay away like this. Is he likely to meet poachers?'

'Let me go and try if I can meet him,' said Oldroyd, jumping up. 'Poachers wouldn't touch him.'

'Yes, do, Mr Oldroyd. I will go with you,' cried Lucy, forgetting in her excitement that such a proposal was hardly etiquette. But neither mother nor daughter, in their anxiety, seemed to have the slightest idea of there being anything extraordinary at such a time.

'It won't do,' Oldroyd had been saying to himself, 'even if it should prove that I'm not a conceited ass to think such things, and she—bless her sweet, bright little face—ever willing to think anything of me, I should be a complete scoundrel to try and win her. Let me see, what did I make last year by my practice? Twenty-eight pounds fifteen, and nine pounds of it still owing, and likely to be owing, for I shall never get a sou. Then this year, what shall I take? Well, perhaps another five pounds on account of her brother's illness. I must be mad.'

'Yes,' he said, after a pause, 'I must be mad, and must have been worse to come down here to this out-of-the-way place, where there is not the most remote chance of my getting together a practice. No, it won't do, I must play misogynist, and be as cold towards the bright little thing as if I were a monk.'

As these thoughts ran through his mind, others came to crowd them out—thoughts of a snug little home, made bright by a sweet face looking out from door or window to see him coming back after a long, tiring round. What was enough for one was enough for two—so people argued. That was right enough as regarded a house, but doubtful when it came to food, and absurd if you went as far as clothing.

'No, it would never do,' he said to himself, 'I could not take her from her home to my poor, shabby place.'

But as he thought this he involuntarily looked round Mrs Alleyne's dining-room, that lady being at the window, and he could not help thinking that, after all, his cottage-like home was infinitely preferable to this great, gaunt, dingy place, where anything suggestive of any comfort was out of the question.

'Yes, she would be more comfortable,' he muttered ; 'and—there, I'm going mad again. I will not think such things.'

Just then Lucy came in ready for starting, and all Philip Oldroyd's good intentions might have been dressed for departure as well. Certainly, they all took flight, as he followed the eager little maiden into the hall.

'Pray—pray let me have news of him directly you find him, Mr Oldroyd,' cried Mrs Alleyne, piteously. 'Run back yourself. You cannot tell what I suffer. Something must have happened.'

'You shall know about him directly, Mrs Alleyne,' replied Oldroyd. 'But pray make your mind easy, nothing can have happened to him here. The worst is that he may have gone to the Hall.'

'No, he would not have gone there without first letting me know.'

'Don't come to the gate, mamma,' cried Lucy. 'There, go in; Mr Oldroyd will take care of me, and we'll soon bring the truant back, only pray be satisfied. Come, Mr Oldroyd, let us run.'

The next minute they were outside the gate, and hurrying down the slope to the common, over whose rugged surface Lucy walked so fast that Oldroyd had to step out boldly. Here the sandy road was reached, and they went on, saying but little, wanting to say but little, for, in spite of all, there was a strange new ecstatic feeling in Lucy's bosom; while, in spite of his honesty something kept whispering to Oldroyd that it would be very pleasant if they were unable to find Alleyne for hours to come.

He was not to be gratified in this, though, for at the end of a quarter of an hour's walking, when they came opposite to the big clump of pines, Lucy proposed that they should go up there.

'I know how fond he is of this place,' she said,

rather excitedly; 'and as its clearer now, I should not be at all surprised to find him here watching the moon, or the rising of some of the stars.'

'We'll go if you wish it,' said Oldroyd, 'but it seems a very unlikely place at a time like this.'

'Ah, but my brother is very curious about such things,' said Lucy, as she left the road, and together they climbed up till all at once she uttered a faint cry—

'Look! there—there he is!'

'Why, Alleyne! Is that you?' cried Oldroyd, as in the full moonlight they saw a dark figure rise from the foot of a pine, and then come slowly towards them silently, and in the same vacant fashion as one in a dream.

'Moray, why don't you speak?' cried Lucy, piteously. 'Why, you've not been to sleep, have you?' and she caught his arm.

'Sleep?' he said, in a strangely absent manner.

'Yes, asleep? Poor mamma has been fretting herself to death about you, and thinking I don't know what. Make haste.'

'Are you unwell, Alleyne?' said Oldroyd, quietly; and the other looked at him wistfully.

'No—no,' he said at length; 'quite well—quite well. I have been thinking—that is all. Let us make haste back.'

Lucy and Oldroyd exchanged meaning glances, and then the former bit her lip, angry at having seemed to take the young doctor into her confidence ; and after that but little was said till they reached The Firs, where Mrs Alleyne was pacing the hall, ready to fling her long, thin arms round her son's neck, and hold him in her embrace as she tenderly reproached him for the anxiety he had caused.

'She doesn't seem to trouble much about little Lucy,' thought the doctor. 'Well, so much the more easy for any one who wanted her for a wife.'

'That couldn't be me,' he said, at the end of a few minutes, and then—

'I wonder what all this means about Alleyne. He must have been having an interview with someone in that Grove. Miss Day, for a hundred. Humph ! She must have said something he did not like, or he would not look like this.'

Then, to the great satisfaction of all, the doctor took his leave, and walked home declaring he would not think of Lucy any more, with the result that the more he strove, the more her pleasant little face made itself plain before him, her eyes looking into his, and illustrating the book he tried to read on every page with a most remarkable sameness, but a repetition that did not tire him in the least.

CHAPTER IV.

A COLLISION.

MRS ROLPH did not see much of her son, who divided his time between Brackley and Aldershot, when he was not away to attend some athletic meeting. But she was quite content, and paid her calls upon Glynne in company with Marjorie, who sat and beamed upon Sir John's daughter, and lost not an opportunity for getting her arm about the waist of her cousin's betrothed, being so intensely affectionate that Glynne stared at her wonderingly at times, and then tried to reciprocate the love bestowed upon her, failed dismally, and often asked Lucy whether she liked Miss Emlin? to receive a short, sharp shake of the head in return.

'Sha'n't say,' Lucy replied one day. 'If I do, you'll think I'm jealous.'

Rolph was not aware of the fact, for Marjorie generally avoided him, and behaved as if she were putting the past farther back; but all the same, she watched her cousin furtively on every possible occasion whenever he was at home or staying at Brackley; and to cover her proceedings, she developed an intense love

39

for botany, and more than once encountered Major Day with Lucy and Glynne, and compared notes. But the major never displayed any great desire to impart information, or to induce the young lady to take up his particular branch.

'Pity Rolph didn't marry her,' muttered the old man. 'Foxy doesn't like Glynne at all.'

Madge's botanical studies had a good deal to do with the *gynias*, and with watching Rolph, who was not aware that his pleasant vices were making of themselves the proverbial rods to scourge him, and unfortunately injure others as well. For Marjorie's brain was busy; and as she watched him, she made herself acquainted with every movement, noting when he rode over to Brackley or took a walk out into the woods—walks which made her writhe, for she gave her cousin the credit of making his way toward Lindham, out by the solitary collection of houses on the road to nowhere, the spot where Ben Hayle had made his new home.

At these times Marjorie hung upon the tenterhooks of agony and suspense till he returned, when there was a warm glow of satisfaction in her breast if his looks showed that his visit had been unsuccessful.

Sometimes though, she was stung by her jealousy into believing that he obtained interviews with Judith, for he would come back looking more satisfied and content.

She watched him one day, and saw him take the path down through the wood, and she also watched his return.

In a few days he went again in the same direction ; and on the next morning she started off before he had left the house, and turned down through the woods to an opening miles away, where, in happier days, she had been wont to gather blackberries; and here she knew she could easily hide in the sandy hollows, and see anyone going toward Lindham—herself unseen.

It was a lonely nook, where, in bygone days, a number of the firs had been cut down, and a sand-pit, or rather sand-pits had been formed. These had become disused, the rabbits had taken possession, and, as sun and air penetrated freely, a new growth of furze, heather and broom grew up among the hollows and knolls.

What her plans were she kept hidden, but a looker-on would have said that she had carefully prepared a mine, and that some day, she would spring that mine upon her cousin with a result that would completely overturn his projects, but whether to her own advantage remained to be seen.

As Marjorie approached, the rabbits took flight, and their white tails could be seen disappearing into their burrows, a certain sign that no one had been by before her ; and in a few minutes she was safely ensconced in a deep hollow surrounded by brambles, after she had taken the precaution to lay a few fern leaves in the bottom of a little basket, and rapidly pick a few weeds to give colour to her presence there.

The time glided on, and all was so still that a stone-chat came and sat upon a twig close at hand, watching her curiously. Then the rabbits stole out one by one from their burrows, and began to race here and there, indulging in playful bounds as if under the impression that it was evening ; but though Marjorie strained her ears to listen, there was no sound of approaching steps, and at last she sat there with her brow full of lines, and her eyes staring angrily from beneath her contracted brows.

'He will not come to-day,' she muttered. 'What shall I do?'

'Oh!' she cried, in a harsh whisper, after a long pause, as she crushed together the nearest tuft of leaves, 'I could kill her.'

She winced slightly, and then glanced contemptuously at her glove, which was torn, and in three places her white palm was pierced, scratched and bleeding, for she had grasped a twig or two of bramble.

The blood on her hand seemed to have a peculiar fascination for her, and she sat there with her eyes half-shut, watching the long red lines made by snatching her hand away, and at the two tiny beads, which gradually increased till she touched them in turn with the tip of her glove, and then carelessly wiped them away.

'"He cometh not,"' she said to herself, with a curious laugh.

Rap! And then, from different parts of the hollow, came the same sharp, clear sound, as rabbit after rabbit struck the ground with its foot, giving the alarm and sending all within hearing scuttling into their holes.

Marjorie had been long enough in the country to know the meaning of that noise, and, with her eyes now wide and wild-looking, she listened for the step which had startled the little animals—one plain to them before it grew clear to her.

No step. Not a sound, and her face was a study, could it have been seen, in its intense eagerness for what seemed, in the silence, minutes, while she retained her breath.

'Hah!'

One long, weary exclamation, and a bitter look of disappointment crossed her eager face.

The next moment it was strained again, and her eyes flashed like those of some wild animal whose life depends upon the acuteness of its perceptions.

There was a faint rustle.

Then silence.

Then a faintly-heard scratching noise, as of a thorn passing over a garment.

'He's coming,' thought Marjorie, 'coming, and this way ; ' and she leaned forward in time to see a figure, bent down so low that it seemed to be going on all fours, dart silently from behind one clump of brambles away to her left, and glide into the shelter of another.

So silently was this act performed that for the moment the watcher asked herself if she had not been deceived.

The answer came directly in the re-appearance of the figure, gliding into sight and creeping on till it was in shelter, hiding not a dozen yards from where she crouched ; and she shrank back with her heart beginning to beat heavily, while she knew that the blood was coming and going in her cheeks.

'No ; I'm not afraid of Caleb Kent,' she thought to herself ; and her eyes flashed again, and in imagination she seemed to see once more the opening where the lodge stood. Her face grew pale, and a curious shrinking sensation attacked her as she recalled Rolph's face, his eyes searching hers with such a bitter look of contempt and scorn.

Then instantly she seemed to be gazing at herself in the library, clinging to her cousin, till he violently wrenched himself from her, leaving her hopeless and crushed ; and she longed bitterly for the opportunity to make some one suffer for this.

'No,' she said to herself, 'I am not afraid of Caleb

Kent ;' and she crouched there, seeing every movement, and in a few moments realised that some one
must be coming, for, with the activity of a cat, the
young half-gipsy, half-poacher, began to move softly
back, as if to keep the clump of brambles between
him and whoever it was that was passing.

Marjorie knew directly after that this must be the
case, for she could hear the dull sound of a step, and
she strained forward a little to try and see, but shrank
back again with her heart beginning to beat rapidly,
as she realised that, all intent upon the person passing in front, Caleb Kent had no thought for what
might be behind, and he had begun to back rapidly
away from the clump which had hidden him, to hide
in the safer refuge already occupied.

She knew that the step must be her cousin's,
and that he was going over to Lindham to seek
Judith.

'Suppose,' she asked herself, 'he should come nearer,
and see her hiding—apparently in company with
Caleb Kent—what would he say?'

She quivered with rage and mortification, and for
the moment felt disposed to spring up and walk away,
but refrained, for she knew that it would then seem
as if she had been keeping an appointment with this
man, and had been frightened into showing herself
by her cousin's coming.

The situation was horrible, and she knew that all
she could do was to wait in the hope that, as soon

as Rolph had gone by, Caleb would glide after him.

'What for?' she asked herself; and she turned cold at the answering thought.

He seemed to have no stout bludgeon, though. Perhaps he was only acting the spy; and as soon as Rolph had been to the cottage and returned, Caleb himself might have some intention of going there.

Marjorie's eyes glittered again as thought after thought came, boding ill to those she hated now with the bitterness of a jealous woman; and all at once, like a flash, a thought flooded her brain which sent the blood thrilling through every artery and vein.

'No,' she thought, and she crouched there, compressing her nether lip between her white teeth. Then,—'Why not? What is she that she should rob me of my happiness, and of all I hold dear? But if—'

She drew in her breath with a faint hiss that was almost inaudible, but it was sufficient to make the poacher pause and look sharply to right and left, as he still crept backwards till he was beneath the shelter of the clump in the hollow which hid Marjorie, and within a few yards of where she was seated.

The sounds of passing steps were very near now. Then there was a faint cough, and Marjorie knew that her cousin was so close that, if he looked about him, he must see her in hiding with this vagabond of the village ; and again the girl's veins tingled with the nervous sensation of anger and mortification.

She would have given ten years of her life to have been back at home ; but she had brought all this upon herself, and she could only hope that Rolph would pass them without turning his head.

'Yes, go on,' said a low, harsh voice, hardly above a whisper, and Marjorie started as she found herself an involuntary listener to the man's outspoken thoughts. 'Only wait,' he continued, and he, too, drew in his breath with a low, hissing sound.

The footsteps died completely away, and Marjorie sat there trembling. The thoughts which had seemed to electrify her, she felt now that she dare not foster ; and she was longing for the man to go, when, as if he were influenced by her presence, he turned round suddenly to the right as in search of some one, then to the left, and, not satisfied, faced right about, his countenance full of wonderment and dread, which passed away directly, and he uttered a low, mocking laugh.

Marjorie shrank away for the moment, but, feeling that she must show no dread of this man who had surprised her in a situation which it would be vain to explain, she rose to go, but Caleb seized her tightly by the arm.

'He did not come to meet you,' the man said, with a look of malicious enjoyment, as if it was a pleasure to inflict some of the pain from which he suffered.

'What do you mean?' she cried imperiously, as she sought to release her wrist.

'Call to him to come back and help you,' whispered Caleb.—'Why don't you?'

He laughed again as he drew himself up into a kneeling position, still holding her tightly,

'How dare you!' cried the girl, indignantly 'Loose my arm, fellow!'

'Why? Not I. You will not call out for fear the captain there should think you were watching to see him go to Hayle's cottage and pretty Judith.'

He began his speech in a light, bantering way, but as he finished his face was flushed and angry, and his breath came thick and fast, while, still clutching the arm he held, he wrenched his head round and knelt there, gazing in the direction taken by Rolph.

The thought which had held possession of Marjorie's breast twice, now came back with renewed power, and, casting all feeling of dread to the winds as she read her companion's face, she snatched at the opportunity.

That Caleb hated Rolph was plain enough; there was a scar upon his lip now that had been made by the hand of one whom he feared as well as hated;

and above all, after his fashion, Marjorie knew that
he loved Judith.

Here was the instrument to her hand. Why had
she not thought of making use of it before?

It was as if she were for the moment possessed, as,
without trying now to release herself, she leaned
forward and whispered in the young man's ear,—

'You coward!'

He turned upon her in astonishment.

'I say you are a coward,' she repeated. 'Why do
you let him go and take her from you?'

There was an animal-like snap of the teeth, as he
snarled out,—

'Why do you let him go?'

'Because I am a woman. I am not a man, and
strong like you.'

'Curse him! I'll kill him,' he snarled.

'What good would that do?'

'Eh?'

'If I were a man like you, do you know how I
would act?'

'No,' he said; 'how could I?' and his lips parted,
to show his white teeth in a peculiar laugh, before
he gave a quick look to right and left, to satisfy himself that they were not seen.

'I'd have revenge.'

'How? With a gun?'

'And be hung for murder. No!'

She leaned towards him, and she too gave a

furtive look round, as, with her face flushed strangely, she whispered a few words to him—words that he listened to with his eyes half closed, and then he turned upon her quickly.

'Why? To bring him back to you?' he said, with a mocking laugh. 'You love him?'

'I hate him,' she said slowly.

'Yes,' he said; 'and you hate Judy Hayle, too, like the gipsy women hate sometimes. Why don't you stop it?'

'Because I am helpless,' she said bitterly. 'Loose my arm. I knew it: you are a coward.'

'Am I?' he said, with an ugly smile. 'Is this a trap?'

'If you think so, let it be,' she said contemptuously; and she tried again to shake her arm free, but the grasp upon it tightened.

'Perhaps I am a coward,' he said; 'but I will. He wouldn't marry her then, and it would be serving him out. Not for nothing, though,' he added, with a laugh. 'What will you give me?'

'Pah!' she said contemptuously; 'how much do you want?'

He laughed and leaned forward, gazing full in her face.

'Perhaps I shall get into trouble again for it,' he said, 'and be shut up for a year—perhaps for more. It's to play your game as well as mine, and I must be paid well.'

'Well, I will pay you,' she said. 'Tell me what you want.'

'A kiss,' he said ; and before she could realise what he had said, his left arm was about her waist, and he held her tightly to him. 'A kiss from a lady who is handsomer than Judy Hayle,' he whispered.

'How dare you !' she cried, in a low voice.

'No,' he said, laughing, 'you won't call for help. Come, it isn't much to give me, and I swear I will.'

Marjorie gazed at him wildly, as she realised her position ; there, alone, in this man's power, and no one at hand to defend her. Then, utterly careless of herself, as she thought of the bitter revenge she had planned, she held back her face, and, with a faint laugh and her voice trembling, she said,—

'No, I will not call for help. There is no need. Keep your word and I will pay you—as you wish.'

The blood crimsoned her cheeks as she spoke

'No,' he said, with a laugh; 'you shall pay me now,' and the next moment his arms were fast round her, and his lips pressed to hers.

Marjorie started away, angry and indignant, but her furious jealousy made her diplomatise, and she stood smiling at the good-looking, gipsy-like ne'er-do-weel, and said laughingly,—

'That was not fair ; I promised you that as a reward, and now you have cheated me and will not keep your word.'

'Yes, I will,' he cried, as he seized her again eagerly; but she kept him back. 'I'll do anything you ask me. Curse Judith Hayle! She isn't half so beautiful as you.'

Madge's heart beat heavily, for admiration was pleasant, even from this low-class scoundrel. His words were genuine, as she could see from his eager gaze, the play of his features, and the earnestness in his voice.

'I've made a slave,' she said to herself, forgetting for a moment the cost, 'and he'll do everything I bid him.'

'Don't talk nonsense,' she said, playfully. 'You do not suppose I believe what you say.'

'What!' he cried, in a low, excited whisper, 'not believe me. Here, tell me anything else to do. Why, I'd kill anyone if you'll look at me like that.'

'I do not want you to kill anyone, and do not want you even to look or speak to me again if you are so rude as that. You forget that I am a lady.'

'No, I don't,' he cried, as he feasted on her with his eyes. 'You're lovely. I never saw a girl so beautiful as you are before.'

He tried to catch her in his embrace again, but she waved him off.

'There,' she said coldly, 'that will do. I see I must ask someone else to do what I want.'

'No, no, don't,' he whispered. 'I didn't mean

to make you cross. I didn't want to offend you, but when you looked at me like you did, with your shiny eyes, I couldn't help myself. I was obliged.'

'Silence! How dare you,' she cried indignantly, as, with her heart throbbing with delight, she felt how very strong a hold she was getting upon Caleb's will. 'You forget yourself, sir.'

'No, I don't; its only because—because—you're so handsome. There, be cross with me if you like. I couldn't help it.'

'And now I suppose you will go and boast in the village taproom that you met the captain's cousin, and insulted her out in the wood.'

'Do you think I'm a fool, miss?' he said sharply. 'Do you think I'd ever go and tell on a girl? Why, I shouldn't tell on a common servant or a farmer's lass, let alone on a handsome lady like you.'

'I don't believe you,' she said, half turning away.

'Yes, do, miss, please do,' he cried earnestly, 'you may trust me. I'd sooner go and hang myself than tell anybody—there!'

She turned her eyes upon him, and her feeling of delight increased as she realised the truth of all that Caleb said. Then, as he looked up at her now, with the appealing, beseeching aspect of a dog in his countenance, she made a pretence of hesitating.

'No,' she said. 'I'm afraid I cannot trust you.'

'Yes, do, miss, do.'

'If I do you will insult me again.'

'I didn't know it was insulting of you to love you,' he said sullenly.

'Then I tell you it was, sir. If you had waited it would have been different.'

He did not speak, but she could see that he was still feasting upon her with his eyes, and the worship in his looks was pleasant after Rolph's cold rebuffs.

'Well,' she cried, 'why are you looking at me like that?'

He started and smiled.

'I can't help it,' he said, 'You are so different to every other girl I know.'

'Except Judith Hayle,' she said contemptuously.

'You're not like her a bit,' he said thoughtfully. 'She's very nice looking, and I used to think a deal of her.'

'Oh, yes, she's lovely,' said Madge with a spiteful laugh.

'Yes,' said Caleb, thoughtfully, 'so she is,' and he stood looking at the girl without comprehending the sarcasm in her words. 'But she hasn't got eyes like you have, and she isn't so white, and,' he whispered, approaching her more closely, 'if you'll only be kind to me, and smile at me like you did, and speak soft to me, I'll be like your dawg.'

He looked as if he would, and Marjorie saw it. She had been on the watch, expecting that he would seize her again, but nothing seemed further from his thoughts. It was exactly as he said—he was ready to be like her dog, and had she told him then, he would have cast himself at her feet, and let her plant her foot upon his neck in token of his subjugation.

'Well,' she said, ' I think I will trust you.'

'You will?' he cried.

'Yes, if you are obedient, and promise me that you will never dare to be so rude again.'

'I'll promise anything,' he cried huskily, ' but—'

'But what, sir?'

'You'll keep your word and pay me?' he said with a laugh.

'Wait and see,' she said indifferently. 'I am going back now.'

'But how am I to tell you?' he said.

'I shall be sure to know.'

'And how shall I see you again?'

'You will not want to see me again,' she said archly.

'Not want to see you,' he whispered. 'Why, I'd go round the world, across the seas, anywhere, to hear you talk to me, and look at your eyes. Tell me when I shall see you again.'

'Oh, I don't know,' she said carelessly, 'perhaps some fine day you'll see me walking in the wood.'

'Yes—yes,' he said eagerly. 'I'll always be about watching for you as I would for a hare.'

'One of my cousin's,' she said, with a contemptuous laugh.

'They're not his,' cried Caleb, quietly, 'they're wild beasts, and as much mine as anybody's.'

'We will not discuss that,' she said coldly. 'Good-bye, and I hope you will keep your word.'

'I've sweared it to myself,' he said, 'and I shall do it. Don't go yet.'

'Why not?' :

'Because I could stand and look at you, like, all day, and it will not seem the same when you are gone.'

'Why, I thought you were a poacher.'

'Well, I suppose I am. What o' that?'

'You talk quite like a courtier?'

'Do I?' he said eagerly. 'Well, you did it; you made me like you.'

'I?'

'Yes. I don't know how it was, but you've made me feel as if I'd do anything for you.'

'Ah, well, we shall see,' said Marjorie, as she fixed her eyes on his, glorying in her triumph, and feeling that every word spoken was the honest truth. Then, giving him a careless nod, she was turning away.

'Don't go like that,' said Caleb, huskily.

'What do you mean?'

'Say one kind word to me first.'

'Well,' said Madge, showing her white teeth in a contemptuous smile, as his eyes were fixed upon hers, just as her cousin's Gordon setter's had been a score of times. 'Poor fellow, then,' she said mockingly, and she held out her little hand, as she would have stretched it forth to pat one of the dogs.

He took it in his brown, sinewy fingers, bent over it, and held it against his cheek. Then, quick as lightning, he had grasped it with a grip like steel, snatched her from where she stood, and almost before she could notice it, he was holding her in a crouching position down behind the bushes, one arm tightly about her waist, and his right hand over her mouth.

She was too much taken by surprise for the moment to struggle or attempt to cry out. Then, as her eyes were fixed upon him fiercely, she felt his hot breath upon her cheek, and his lips pressed upon her ear.

'Don't move, don't speak,' whispered the man, 'he mustn't see you along o' me.'

Madge strained her sense of hearing, but all was perfectly still, and, concluding that it was a trick, she gathered herself together for a strong effort to get free, when there was a sharp crack as of a broken twig. Then the low brushing sound of dead strands of grass against a man's leg; and, directly after Rolph came into view, plainly seen through the brambles, and as he came nearer Marjorie grew faint.

If he should see her—like that—clasped in this man's arms!

Rolph came nearer and nearer, his way leading him

so close to where his cousin crouched that it seemed
impossible that he could go by without seeing her,
held there by a man whom he would look upon as
the scum of the earth. The agony of shame and
mortification she suffered was intense, the greater because her presence here was due to the fact that she
had vowed that, in spite of all, she would yet be
Rolph's wife, the mistress of The Warren.

As her cousin came on, and she felt Caleb's arm
tightening about her, a strange giddiness made her
brain swim, and the objects about her grew misty;
but clearly seen in advance of this mist was her
cousin's face, his eyes fixed upon the very spot where
she was hiding, and plunging through the leaves to
search her out, to drag her forth and upbraid her with
being a disgrace to her sex, a woman utterly lost to
all sense of shame. And all the time, throb, throb,
throb, with heavy beat, she could feel Caleb Kent's
heart, and a twitching sensation in the muscle of his
arm, as, influenced by the man's thoughts of flight or
violence, he loosened his grip, or held her more tightly
still.

'He must see us,' thought Marjorie. 'Oh, if I
could only die!'

Close up now, and as he came nearer Rolph struck
sharply with his stick at a loose strand which pro-
jected half across his path.

He must see them; he could not help seeing them,
thought Marjorie; and then her heart stood still, and

the mist began to close her in, for, to her horror, the culmination of her shame seemed to have arrived. Rolph stopped short, leaned over, apparently to part the brambles and gaze through them at the hiding pair, and then muttered something half aloud as he reached over more and more till his face was not six feet from his cousin's, staring up at him with her eyes full of horror.

A guilty conscience needs no accuser; so runs the old proverbial saying.

Rolph had caught sight of an extra large blackberry and he had reached out and picked it, more from habit, fostered by a country life, than desire, and then passed on.

A long time appeared to elapse, during which Marjorie lay listening to steps which thundered upon her ear, before a voice, that sounded as if it came from far away, whispered,—

'It's all right, now. I don't think he saw.'

Marjorie looked at the speaker strangely, and then turned away, plunging into the thickest part of the wood to try and grow calm before making her way home, and in perfect unconsciousness of the fact that, not twenty yards away, Caleb Kent was following her, gliding from tree to tree, and always keeping her in sight.

Sometimes she stopped to rest her hand upon one of the pine trunks, apparently wrapt in thought; and Caleb Kent drew a long breath and told himself that she was thinking about him. Then she walked swiftly on again till she was at the very edge of the wood, where she stepped down into the sandy lane where he could not follow ; but, quickly, almost as a squirrel, he mounted a tall spruce by its short, dense, ladder-like branches, to where, high up, he could still keep the girl in sight, elated by his adventure, and little thinking that she was asking herself whether it would be very difficult to kill Caleb Kent next time she met him in the woods, and so silence for ever a tongue whose utterances might ruin her beyond recovery.

'Something to drink—something to drink,' she kept on thinking. 'To drink my health.'

Her eyes brightened, and her strange look told of an excitement within her which made every pulse throb and bound.

'It would be so easy,' she said to herself. But the feeling of elation passed away as she recalled the man's furtive, suspicious nature, and, in imagination, saw him fixing his keen eyes upon her, and asking her to drink first.

CHAPTER V.

THE SETTING OF A DOG'S STAR.

THE gentlemen were seated over their claret at the Hall, and the party had become very quiet. Sir John had been preaching on the subject of the value of a cross of the big, coarse, wool-bearing Lincolnshire sheep with the Southdown, as being likely to prove advantageous, the Lincolnshire sheep giving increased wool-bearing qualities, while the lamb would inherit the fine properties of its mother's mutton.

At the words mutton and Southdown lamb, Rolph had pricked up his ears for a moment, since they had suggested under-done chops and cuts out of good haunches, with the gravy in grand supplies of stamina to an athlete; but the suggestion came at the wrong end of the dinner, and, with a yawn, the captain had wished Sir John and his pigs and sheep at Jericho, and begun thinking of his coming match with the Bayswater Stag for a hundred pounds a side, a race for which he told himself he was in training now, though his proceedings in the way of wines and foods would have horrified a trainer and frightened his backers into fits of despair.

When Sir John had had his innings, the major began to talk about the translation of a paper by Friés, on the persistency of certain forms of parasitic fungi in the lower plants. To make himself a little more comprehendible to his companions, he kept introducing the word mushroom into his discourse, with the effect of bringing back Rolph's wandering attention, and rousing Sir John from the doze into which he was falling.

Both gentlemen saw mushrooms directly, through a medium of claret, and while the major was thinking of spores, mycelium, and rapid generation, Sir John and the captain saw mushrooms growing, mushrooms cooked, mushrooms in rich sauces, but always of a deep purply claret colour, that was pleasant to the eye.

'Hang 'em, they'll drive me mad between 'em,' thought Rolph. 'I wonder how much of this sort of thing a man could stand. Offend the old buffers or no, I must go and have a cigar.'

'Yes, what is it?' said Sir John, starting out of a doze.

'Morton would like to speak to you, Sir John.'

'Morton; what does he want?' said Sir John. 'Send him in.'

A good deal of shoe wiping was heard outside, and a fine-looking, elderly man, whose velveteens proclaimed his profession, entered, to bow to all three gentlemen in turn.

'Sorry to trouble you, Sir John, but I've got information that a party from out Woodstay way, sir, are
coming netting and snaring to-night.'

'Con—found their impudence!' cried Sir John,
leaping from his chair. 'What the deuce do you
mean, standing staring there like a fool, man? Why
don't you get the helpers and the watchers together,
and go and stop the scoundrels?'

'Men all waiting, Sir John,' said the keeper, quietly,
'but I thought you and the captain would like to be
there, and the major could give us a bit of advice as
to plans, Sir John.'

'Quite right, Morton. Of course. Quite right.
Take a glass of wine. Here's a claret glass. You
won't have claret though, I suppose.'

'Thank ye, kindly, Sir John, but you give me a
glass of port last time.'

'And you haven't forgotten it, Morton? Quite
right. It's a fine port. Help yourself, man. We'll
change, and be with you directly. You'll come,
Rolph?'

'By George, yes,' cried the captain, whose face had
flushed with excitement. 'I'm ready there.'

'You'll come, Jem?'

'To be sure—to be sure,' said the major, rubbing
his hands. 'We'll have a bit of tactics here.'

Ten minutes later, Sir John and the major, each
carrying a heavy staff, and Rolph, armed with a gun,
were following the keeper along one of the paths

leading to the fir woods, and with a great mastiff dog close at the keeper's heels.

'Beg pardon, sir,' said the keeper, touching his hat, as they drew near to where a knot of men were gathered waiting for them, 'but I wouldn't use that gun.'

'Oh, it's only loaded with No. 7, Morton,' said the captain. 'I sha'n't fire; but if I did, it would only pepper them.'

The man drew back, muttering to himself, 'I saw a chap shot dead with No. 7, and they wasn't chilled shot, neither. I've done my duty, though.'

There were six men waiting, all armed with short staves, and looking a steady set of fellows as Sir John cast his eye over them, and now increased to ten by the coming of the little party from the Hall, they looked more than a match for any gang of poachers likely to be met, and he said so.

'I don't know, Sir John,' said the keeper, sturdily. 'I haven't much faith in 'em. If it warn't for the show they'll make, I'd as soon trust to you, Sir John, the major, the captain, and Nero here. They're safe to run, some of 'em, if it comes to a fight. That chap of the captain's, Thompson, has got arms like pipe shanks, and two of the helpers about as much pluck as a cuckoo.'

'Oh, they'll fight if it comes to the proof, I daresay,' said Sir John. 'How are you, my lads; how are you?' he continued, as they came up. 'Now, then, if we come across the scoundrels, we must take all we can. There's no excuse for poaching. I'd give any man out of work in the parish something to do on the farm. So it's as bad as stealing, and I'll have no mercy on them. Now, Morton, what are you going to do?'

'Well, Sir John, from what I can understand, they're coming with their nets and dogs to scour the meadows and the cut clover patches. There's a sight of young birds there, as I know. They've got to know of it, too, somehow; and I propose, if the major thinks it right, to 'vide ourselves in three. You and me, Sir John, with one man and the dog, and the major and the captain take the other two parties, and lay up till we see 'em come.'

'But how shall we know which way they'll come?' said Sir John.

'They'll come over the common from Woodstay way, Sir John, through the fir wood, and down at once into the long meadow, safe. We'll take one side, the major the other, and Captain Rolph the bottom of the meadow. We'll let them get well to work, and then when I whistle all close in, and get as many of 'em as we can. We shall be sure of their nets anyhow, but when I whistle they'll scatter, and I don't suppose we shall catch more'n one or two.'

'Capital plan,' said the major. 'Why, you would have made a good general, Morton.'

'Thank ye, sir,' said the keeper, touching his hat.
'All ready there?   Long Meadow.'

It was a soft, dark night, with not a breath of wind
to chase the heavy clouds that shrouded the sky.
There was no talking—nothing to be heard but the
dull tramp of feet, and the rustling noise made by
the herbage and heather brushing against the leather
leggings worn by the men who followed the lead of
the keeper and his dog.

There was about half a mile to go to reach the indi-
cated spot, and the blood of both Rolph and the
major seemed to course a little more rapidly through
their veins as the one hailed the prospect of a bit of
excitement with something like delight, and the other
recalled night marches and perilous episodes in his
old Indian campaigning life, and then sighed as he
compared his present elderly self with the smart,
dashing young officer he used to know.

'Halt here!' said Sir John, interrupting the musings
of his brother; and from where they stood, they could
dimly make out the extent of the long open space,
with fir plantations on either side, a patch of alder in
the damp, boggy space where they stood, and about
two hundred yards away, right at the top of the
slight slope, there was something black to be seen
against the sky—something black, that by daylight
would have resolved itself into a slope of tall firs.

This was the part that the poachers were expected
to traverse, and the three parties were therefore

stationed according to the plan, and for three hours they waited in utter silence, hidden in the plantations and the alder clump.

Sir John had begun to mutter at the end of the first hour, to grumble at the end of the second, and he was growling fiercely at the end of the third, when the keeper suddenly started up.

'What is it?' said Sir John, as the dog uttered a low whine.

'They've circumvented us, Sir John,' replied the keeper, angrily. 'They've trapped me into the belief that they were coming here to-night, and they've been netting Barrows, I'll be bound.'

'Confound the scoundrels!' cried Sir John. 'What an idiot you must have been!'

'Yes, Sir John, I was,' said the keeper, calmly; 'but they won't have more than finished, and they've got to get home. I may be too many for them yet.'

Hastily summoning the party on his left, the keeper led them to the weary, cramped party on his right.

'This way; quick!' he said; and the sluggish blood began to flow once more with the excitement, as he led them rapidly along the meadow, right up the fir slope through the trees, and out into the lane on the other side.

Here he paused and listened for a few moments, and then started off once more to where another clump of firs made the aspect of the night more dark.

Beneath the trees it was blacker, but the keeper well knew his way, and at the end of a few minutes he had spread out his forces some fifteen yards apart, with a whispered word to be on the alert.

'They're sure to come through here,' he whispered. ' Down on the first man you see. We shall hear you, and will come and help.'

General like, the keeper had selected the middle of the line for himself, and placed the trustiest men near where he believed that the poachers would come, Rolph being on his right, the major and Sir John upon his left.

'They won't come—it's all a hoax,' said Sir John, who was tired of waiting, and the words were hardly out of his lips before the mastiff uttered a muttered growl, and directly after there was the tramp of feet over the pine needles which, as it came nearer, told plainly of there being a strongish gang at work.

'Sir John's party kept perfectly quiet, save that a couple of the men began to close up so as to be ready when the signal was given, while apparently quite free from apprehension, the poachers came on talking in a low voice, till they were close upon Sir John, when the keeper gave a shrill whistle, sprang up, and shouted to his men.

'Stand back all of you,' cried a stern voice.

'Give up, you scoundrels, the game's over,' cried Sir John. 'Close in, my lads.'

He dashed forward at once, and the major and

keeper well seconded his efforts, but the latter received a heavy blow on the forehead, and went down, felled like an ox, the major was tripped up, and the man whom Sir John attacked proved too much for him, getting him down and kneeling upon his chest.

'Shoot them if they come, and then step forrard,' cried a shrill harsh voice, and four reports followed, the poachers sending the shot rattling in amongst the branches over the watchers' heads, the pine needles and twigs pattering down, and the result was that Thompson, Captain Rolph's man, began to retire very rapidly in one direction, closely followed by two more, and while others from the right flank also beat a retreat.

The scuffle that took place to right and left was soon over, the keeper's followers not caring to risk their lives in an encounter with armed and desperate men. There was the sound of blows and another shot or two from the poachers, who were eight or nine in number, under the guidance of the man who had felled the keeper, and got Sir John down.

'It's all right, my lads,' growled a voice. 'Tie 'em well and let's be off.'

'Here, rope!' said a fresh voice; and then there was another scuffle, as Sir John and the major were forced over on their faces, and their wrists tied behind them.

'Here, help! Rolph, Rolph!' cried Sir John.

'Hold your row, or—'

There was a dull sound like the blow of the butt of a gun on a man's head, and Sir John uttered a furious oath.

'I'll have you before me, yet, you dog!' he cried.

'And commit me for trial then,' said the man with a laugh. 'Not this time. Now, my lads, ready?'

'Ay.'

'Off!'

'Halt!'

There was a fierce murmur at this last command, uttered in a good ringing military voice, and Sir John's heart leaped, and the major thought better of the speaker than he had ever thought before, as they both recognised the voice.

'Down with him, lads, he's only one,' growled another.

'Halt, or by G—d I'll fire,' cried Rolph again.

It all happened in an instant. There was the sound of a blow, which the captain received on his left arm; of another which came full upon his head, and then there was a flash, cutting the darkness and lighting up the faces of a group of men, a ringing report, and a moan, as Rolph fell back heavily to the ground.

What followed was a hurried muttering of voices amid painful, hoarse breathing, and, in the darkness, the major could just make out that men were lifting a burden.

'Who's hurt?' cried Sir John. 'Do you hear?— who's hurt?'

There was no answer, only the trampling of feet rapidly receding ; and it was the major who now spoke.

'Jack,' he cried, 'I can't move ; I'm tied, I'm afraid it's Rolph.'

'God forbid !' groaned Sir John.

'Curse the brutes ! Here, my arm's smashed,' muttered someone, struggling to his feet. 'Hi, Sir John !—Major !'

'You, Rolph ? Thank heaven !' cried Sir John. 'I was afraid you were killed. Where's Morton ?'

'Here, Sir John,' said a faint voice.

'Don't say you're shot, man.'

'No, Sir John. Crack on the head.'

'Then who is hurt ?' said the major. 'Here, some-one, untie or cut this line.'

'I'm a bit hurt,' said Rolph ; 'arm bruised, and a touch on the head, too.'

'But someone must have been shot. Did you fire ?' said Sir John.

'I think I did. Yes,' said Rolph, 'I got a crack on the arm, and I had a finger on the trigger.'

'Then someone is down,' cried Sir John. 'Where are our men ?'

'Gone for help, I think,' said the major drily, as Rolph succeeded in loosening Sir John's hands.

'The cowardly scoundrels !' roared Sir John. 'Here, let's pursue the poachers.'

'No, no,' said the major. 'We're defeated this time, Jack, and they've retired. Thank you, Morton. I think we four made a good fight of it, and—ah, poor fellow!' he cried, bending down. 'Nero, Nero, good dog then.'

In the darkness they could just see the great dog make an effort to reach the major's hand, but the attempt resulted in a painful moan; a shudder, a faint struggle, and death.

'I'll swear it was not my shot killed him,' cried Rolph excitedly.

'Say no more about it,' said Sir John; 'it was an accident. I'd sooner one of the scoundrels had had it in his skin, though. I wouldn't have taken fifty pounds for that dog.'

'Poor old fellow!' said the major, who was kneeling beside the dog, and he stroked the great ears; 'but,' he added softly to himself, 'I've had enough of blood : thank God it was not a man.'

A series of loud whistles brought back some of the scattered forces, the men meeting with such an ovation from Sir John that they began to think they had better have had it out honourably with the poachers ; and then a stout sapling was cut down, and the dog's paws being tied, he was carried home to the stable-yard on the shoulders of two watchers.

After this, there was much beer drinking in the servant's-hall, and much discussion in the library, where a piece of sticking-plaister was sufficient to remedy Rolph's wound, his arm was bathed, and Glynne did not faint.

Rolph soon after retired for the night, the major noting that he was looking very pale and uneasy. Twice over he went and looked at himself in the glass, and once he shuddered and stood staring over his shoulder, as if expecting to see someone there.

'Man can't help his gun going off in the excitement of an action,' he said slowly. 'What a fool I was not to own up that I had shot the big dog.'

'Well, they shouldn't poach,' he muttered at last; and, lighting a cigar, he sat smoking for an hour before going to bed to sleep soundly, awake fairly fresh the next morning, and go out for what he termed 'a breather.'

CHAPTER V.I.

ERRANT COURSES.

LUCY ALLEYNE was very pretty. Everybody said so—that she was pretty. No one said that she was beautiful. Now, Lucy was well aware of what people said, and, without being conceited, she very well knew that what people said was true. In fact, she often admired her pretty little *retroussé* nose and creamy skin in the glass, and, with a latent idea that she ought to preserve her good looks as much as possible for some one. She thought of the favoured person as ' some one,' and tried in every way possible to lead a healthy life.

To attain the above end, she strove hard to improve her complexion. It did not need improving, being perfect in its shades of pink and creamy white, that somehow put him who gazed upon her in mind of a *Gloire de Dijon* rose ; but she tried to improve it all the same, laughingly telling herself that she would wash it in morning dew, or rather let Nature perform the operation, as she went for a good early walk.

The pine woods and copses looked as if trouble

could never come within their shades, and the last thing any one would have dreamed of would have been the possibility of men meeting there with sticks, bludgeons, and guns, ready to resist capture on the one side, to effect it on the other, and, if needs be, use their weapons to the staining of the earth with blood.

No news of the past night's encounter had reached The Firs. Moray Alleyne, while watching the crossing of a star in the zenith over certain threads of cobweb in the field of his transit instrument had heard the reports of guns; but he was too much intent upon his work to pay heed to what was by no means an unusual circumstance. Lucy, too, had started into wakefulness once, thinking she heard a sound, but only to sink back to her rest once more; and as she walked that morning she saw no sign of struggle, though, had she turned off to the right amongst the pines, she might have found one or two ugly traces, as if a burden had had been laid down by those who bore it while they rested for a few minutes, and while a bit of rough surgery was being performed.

The lovely silvery mists were hanging about in the little valleys, or curling around the tops, as if spreading veils over the sombre pines, patches of which, as seen in the early morning sunshine, resembled the dark green and purple plaid of some Scottish clan ; and as Lucy reached the edge of the far-stretching common land, dazzled by the brilliancy of the sum-shine, and elated by the purity of the morning air, she paused to enjoy the beauty of the lovely scene around.

'How stupid people are !' she said half aloud. 'How can they call this place desolate and ugly. Why, there's something growing everywhere, and the gorse and broom are simply lovely.'

There was a soft moisture in her pretty eyes, as they rested on the blue-looking distant hills, the purple stretches of heather, and the rich green lawn-like patches of meadow land, saved from the wilds around. Between the hills there were dark shadowy spots, upon them brilliant bits of sunshine, while on all sides the gauzy, silvery vapours floated low down, waiting for the sun, as it increased in power, to drink them up, and after them the millions of iridescent tiny globules that whitened the herbage like frost.

The birds were singing from every patch of wood-land in the distance; there was the monotonous 'coo coo, coo-*coo*, coo-*hoo*-coo !' of a wood-pigeon in the pine tops singing his love-song that he always ends in the middle, and far out over the heathery common lark after lark was circling round and rising, in a wide spiral, up and up into the blue sky as it poured forth the never-wearying strain.

'People are as stupid and as dense as can be,' said Lucy. 'Ours is a grim-looking home, I know, but oh ! how beautiful the country is—I wouldn't live any-where else for the world.'

'There seemed to be no reason for a blush to come into Lucy's cheeks at this declaration, but one certainly did come, like a ruddy cloud over their soft outline, as she glanced back at the blank-looking pile with the hideous brick additions made by Alleyne for his instruments and observations. Not so much as a thread of smoke rose yet, from either of the chimneys, for Eliza was only at the point that necessitated a vexed rub occasionally at her nose with the woody part of a blacklead brush; Mrs Alleyne was dreaming of her son ; and her son, who sought his pillow a couple of hours before—after a long watch of his star as it climbed to the zenith and then went down—to lie and think of Glynne Day, and ask himself whether he was not a scoundrel to allow such thoughts to enter his breast.

'How good it is to get up so early,' thought Lucy, aloud ; and then she stepped lightly over the dewy grass, marked down the spot where several mushrooms were growing, and then stepped on to the sandy road.

'I wish Moray would get up early,' she thought, 'it would be so nice to have him for a companion ; but, poor fellow, he must be tired of a morning. I know what I'll do,' she cried suddenly. 'I'll get Glynne to promise to meet me two or three times a week, whenever it's fine, and we'll go together.'

Her cheeks flushed a little hot as she began to

think about Glynne, and her thoughts ran somewhat in this fashion,—

'She doesn't know—she doesn't understand a bit, or she would never have consented. Oh! it's absolutely horrid, and I don't believe he cares for her a morsel more than she cares for him.'

Lucy stooped down to pick a mushroom, and laid it aside ready to retrieve as she came back from her walk, for Mrs Alleyne approved of a dish for breakfast.

'Why, at the end of a year it would be horrible,' cried Lucy, with emphasis. 'Mrs Rolph! What would be the use of being married, if you were miserable, as I'm sure she would be.'

'It isn't dishonourable; and if it is, I don't mind. I know he is beginning to worship her, and it's as plain as can be that she likes to sit and listen to him, and all he says about the stars. Why, she seems to grow and alter every day, and to become wiser, and to take more interest in everything he says and does.'

'There, I don't care,' she panted, half-tearfully, as she picked another mushroom; and, as if addressing someone who had had spoken chidingly, 'I can't help it; he is my own dear brother, and I will help him as much as I can. Dishonourable? Not it. It is right, poor fellow! Why, she has come like so much sunshine in his life, and it is as plain as can be to see that she is gradually beginning to know what love really is.'

As these thoughts left her heart, she looked guiltily round, but there was no one listening—nothing to take her attention, but a couple of glistening, wet, and silvery-looking mushrooms in the grass hard by.

'It's very dreadful of me to be thinking like this,' she said to herself, as she finished culling the mushrooms, and began to make her way back to the road, 'but I can't help it. I love Glynne, and I won't see my own brother made miserable, if I can do anything to make him happy. It's quite dreadful the way things are going, and dear Sir John ought to be ashamed of himself. I declare— Oh! how you made me start!'

This was addressed to wet-coated, dissipated rabbit, with a tail like a tuft of white cotton, which little animal started up from its hiding-place at her very feet, and went bounding and scuffling off amongst the heather and furze.

'I wish, oh, how I wish that things would go right,' cried Lucy, with tears in her eyes. 'I wish I could do something to make Glynne see that he thinks ten times more about his nasty races and matches than he does about her. I don't believe he loves her a bit. It's shameful. He's a beast!'

There was another pause, during which the larks went on singing, the wood-pigeon cooed, and there was a pleasant twittering in the nearest plantation.

'Poor Glynne! when she might be so happy with a man who really loves her, but who would die sooner than own to it. Oh, dear me! I wish a dreadful war would break out, and Captain Rolph's regiment be ordered out to India, and the Indians would kill him and eat him, or take him prisoner—I don't care what, so long as they didn't let him come back any more, and—'

Pat—pat —pat —pat —pat —pat —pat —pat — a regular beat from a short distance off, and evidently coming from round by the other side of a clump of larches, where the road curved and then went away level and straight for about a mile.

'Whatever is that?' thought Lucy, whose eyes grew rounder, and who stared wonderingly in the direction of the sound. 'It can't be a rabbit, I'm quite sure.'

She was perfectly right ; it was not a rabbit, as she saw quite plainly the next minute, when a curious-looking figure in white, braided and trimmed with blue, but bare-armed, bare-legged and bare-headed, came suddenly into view, with head forward, fists clenched, and held up on a level with its chest, and running at a steady, well-sustained pace right in the middle of the sandy road.

It was a surprise for both.

'Captain Rolph!' exclaimed Lucy, as the figure stopped short, panting heavily, and looking a good deal surprised.

'Miss Alleyne! Beg pardon. Didn't expect to see anybody so early. Really.'

Lucy felt as if she would like to run away, but that she felt would be cowardly, so she stood her ground, and made, sensibly enough, the best of matters in what was decidedly a rather awkward encounter.

'I often come for an early walk,' said the girl, coolly as to speech, though she felt rather hot. 'Is this—is this for amateur theatricals?'

It would have been wiser not to allude to the captain's costume, but the words slipped out, and they came like a relief to him, for he, too, had felt tolerably confused. As it was his features expanded into a broad grin, and he then laughed aloud.

'Theatricals? Why, bless your innocence, no. I am in training for a race—foot-race—ten miles—man who does it in shortest time gets the cup. I give him—'

'Him?' said Lucy, for her companion had paused.

'Yes, him,' said the captain. 'Champion to run against.'

'Run against?' said Lucy, glancing at a great blue bruise upon the captain's arm and a piece of sticking-plaister upon his forehead. 'Do you hurt yourself like that when you run against men?'

'Haw, haw, haw! Haw, haw, haw!' laughed the captain. 'I beg pardon, but, really, you are such a daisy. So innocent, you know. That was done last night out in the woods. Bit of a row with some poacher chaps. One of them hit me with a stick on the head. That's from the butt of a gun.'

He gave the bruise on his bare arm a slap, and laughed, while Lucy coloured with shame and annoyance, but resolved to ignore the captain's rather peculiar appearance, and escape as soon as she could.

'I ought not to mind,' she said to herself. 'It's only rather French. Like the pictures one sees in the illustrated papers about Trouville.'

'Were you fighting?'

'Well, yes,' he said indifferently, 'bit of a scrimmage. Nothing to mind. People who preserve often meet with that sort of a thing. I did run against a fellow, though,' he continued, laughing. 'But that's not the sort of running against I meant. I'm going to do a foot-race. Matched against a low sort of fellow.'

'Oh!' said Lucy, looking straight before her.

'Professional, you know; but I'm going to run him—take the conceit out of the cad. Bad thing conceit.'

'Extremely,' said Lucy tightening her lips.

'Horrid. I'm going to give him fifty yards.'

'Oh!' said Lucy, gravely, as she took a step forward without looking at the captain. 'But don't let me hinder you. I was only taking my morning walk.'

'Don't hinder me a bit,' said the captain. 'I was

just going to put on the finishing spurt, and end at that cross path. I've as good as done it, and I'm in prime condition.'

'Bad thing conceit,' said Lucy to herself.

'Fresh as a daisy.'

'Horrid,' said Lucy again to herself.

'I feel as if I could regularly run away from him. My legs are as hard as nails.'

'Indeed!'

'Oh, yes. I haven't trained like this for nothing. Don't you think you've hindered me. I sha'n't trouble about it any more.'

All this while Lucy was trying to escape from her companion, but it was rather a wild idea to trudge away from a man whose legs were as hard as nails. As she walked on, though, she found herself wondering whether the finishing spurt that the captain talked of putting on was some kind of garment, as she kept steadily along, with, to her great disgust, the captain keeping coolly enough by her side, and evidently feeling quite at home, beginning to chat about the weather, the advantages of early rising, and the like.

'I declare,' thought Lucy, 'if I met anyone, I should be ready to sink through the ground for shame. I wish he'd go.'

'Some people waste half their days in bed, Miss Alleyne. Glad to see you don't. I've been up these two hours, and feel, as they say, as fit as a fiddle, and, if you'll forgive me for saying so, you look just the same you do really, you know.'

He cast an admiring glance at her, which she noted, and for the moment it frightened her, then it fired a train, and a mischievous flash darted from her eyes.

This was delicious, and though her cheeks glowed a little, perhaps from the exercise, her heart gave a great leap, and began to rejoice.

'I knew he was not worthy of her,' she thought. 'The wretch! I won't run away, though I want to very badly.' And she walked calmly on by his side.

'Don't you find this place dull?' said Rolph.

'Dull? oh dear no,' cried Lucy, looking brightly up in his face, and recalling at the same time that this must be at least the tenth time she had answered this question.

'I wish you'd let my mother call upon you, and you'd come up to the Hall a little oftener, Miss Alleyne, 'pon my honour I do.'

'Why, I do come as often as I am asked, Captain Rolph,' said Lucy with a mischievous look in her eyes.

'Do you, though? Well, never mind, come oftener.'

'Why?' said Lucy, with an innocent look of wonder in her round eyes.

'Why? because I want to see you, you know. It's precious dull there sometimes.'

'What, with Glynne there?' cried Lucy.

'Oh yes, sometimes. She reads so much.'

'Fie, Captain Rolph!'

'No, no; nonsense. Oh, I say, though, I wish you would.'

'Really, Captain Rolph, I don't understand you,' said Lucy, who was in a flutter of fright, mischief and triumph combined.

'Oh yes, you do,' he said 'but hold hard a minute. Back directly.'

He ran from her out to where something was hanging on a broken branch of a pine, and returned directly, putting on a flannel cricketing cap, and a long, hooded ulster, which, when buttoned up, gave him somewhat the aspect of a friar of orders grey, who had left his beads at home.

'You do understand me,' he said, not noticing the mirthful twinkle in Lucy's eye at his absurd appearance. 'Oh yes, you do. It's all right. I say, Lucy Alleyne, what a one you are.'

Lucy's eyebrows went up a little at this remark, but she did not assume displeasure, she only looked at him inquiringly.

'Oh, it's all right,' he said again. 'I am glad I met you, it's so precious dull down here.'

'What, when you have all your training to see to, Captain Rolph.'

'Oh, yes; awfully dull. You see Glynne doesn't take any interest in a fellow's pursuits. She used to at first, but now it's always books.'

'But you should teach her to be interested, Captain Rolph.'

'Oh, I say, hang it all, Lucy Alleyne, can't you drop that captaining of a fellow when we're out here *tête-à-tête.* It's all very well up at the Hall but not here, and so early in the morning, we needn't be quite so formal, eh?'

'Just as you like,' said Lucy, with the malicious twinkle in her eyes on the increase.

'That's right,' cried Rolph; 'and, I say, you know, come, own up—you did, didn't you?'

'Did what?' cried Lucy.

'Know I was training this morning.'

'Indeed, no,' cried Lucy, indignantly, with a look that in no wise abashed the captain.

'Oh, come now, that won't do,' cried Rolph. 'There's nothing to be ashamed of.'

'I'm not a bit ashamed,' cried Lucy stoutly; and then to herself, 'Oh yes, I am—horribly. What a fright, to be sure!'

'That's right,' cried Rolph, 'but I know you did come, and I say I'm awfully flattered, I am, indeed. I wish, you know, you'd take a little more interest in our matches and engagements: it would make it so much pleasanter for a fellow.'

'Would it?' said Lucy.

'Would it? Why, of course it would. You see I should feel more like those chaps used, in the good old times, you know, when they used to bring the wreaths and prizes they had won, and lay 'em at ladies' feet, only that was confoundedly silly, of course. I don't believe in that romantic sort of work.'

'Oh, but that was at the feet of their lady-loves,' said Lucy, quickly.

'Never mind about that,' replied Rolph; 'must have someone to talk to about my engagements. It's half the fun.'

'Go and talk to Glynne, then,' said Lucy.

'That's no use, I tell you. She doesn't care a *sou* for the best bit of time made in anything. Here, I believe,' he said, warmly, 'if that what's-his-name chap, who said he'd put a girdle round the globe in less than no time, had done it, and come back to Glynne and told her so, she'd just lift up her eyes—'

'Her beautiful eyes,' said Lucy, interrupting.

'Oh, yes, she's got nice eyes enough,' said Rolph, sulkily; 'but she'd only have raised 'em for a moment and looked at him, and said—"Have you really." Here, I say, Puck's the chap I mean.'

'I don't think Glynne's very fond of athletic sports,' said Lucy.

'No, but you are; I know you are. Come, it's of no use to deny it. I say I am glad.'

'Why, the monster's going to make love to me,' said Lucy to herself.

'You are now, aren't you?'

'Well, I don't dislike them,' said Lucy; 'not very much.'

'Not you; and, I say, I may talk to you a bit about my engagements, mayn't I?'

'Really, Captain Rolph,' replied Lucy, demurely, 'I hardly know what to say to such a proposal as this. To how many ladies are you engaged?'

'Ladies? Engaged? Oh, come now! I say, you know, you don't mean that. I say, you're chaffing me, you know.'

'But you said engaged, and I knew you were engaged to Glynne Day,' cried Lucy, innocently.

'Oh, but you know I meant engagements to run at athletic meetings. Of course I'm only engaged to Glynne, but that's no reason why a man shouldn't have a bit of a chat to any one else—any one pretty and sympathetic, and who took an interest in a fellow's pursuits. I say, I've got a wonderful match on, Lucy.'

'How dare he call me Lucy!' she thought; and an indignant flash from her eyes fell upon a white-topped button mushroom beside the road. 'A pretty wretch to be engaged to poor Glynne. Oh, how stupid she must be!'

The mushroom was not snatched up, and Rolph went on talking, with his hands far down in the pockets of his ulster.

'It's no end of a good thing, and I'm sure to win. It's to pick up five hundred stones put five yards

apart, and bring 'em back and put 'em in a basket one
at a time; so that, you see, I have to do—twice five
yards is ten yards the first time, and then twice
ten yards the second time; and then twice twenty
yards is forty yards the third time, and then twice
forty yards is eighty yards the fourth time, and—
Here, I say, I'm getting into a knot, I could do it if
I had a pencil.'

' But I thought you would have to run.'

' Yes; so I have. I mean to tot up on a piece of
paper. It's five yards more twice over each time,
you know, and mounts up tremendously before you're
done; but I've made up my mind to do it, and I will.'

' All that's very brave of you,' cried Lucy, looking
him most shamelessly full in the eyes, and keeping
her own very still to conceal the twitching mischief
that was seeking to make puckers and dimples in all
parts of her pretty face.

' Well,' he said, heavily, ' you can't quite call it
brave. It's plucky, though,' he added, with a self-
satisfied smile. ' There are not many fellows in my
position who would do it.'

' Oh, no, I suppose not,' said Lucy, with truthful
earnestness this time; and then to herself: ' He's
worse than I thought.'

' Now that's what I like, you know,' exclaimed
Rolph. ' That's what I want—a sort of sympathy,
you know. To feel that when I'm doing my best to
win some cup or belt there's one somewhere who

takes an interest in it, and is glad for me to win.   Do
you see?'

'Oh, of course I am glad for you to win, if it pleases
you,' said Lucy, demurely.

'But it doesn't please me if it doesn't please you,'
cried Rolph.   'I've won such a heap of times, that I
don't care for it much, unless there should be some
one I could come and tell about it all.'

'Then why not tell Glynne?' said Lucy, opening
her limpid eyes, and gazing full in the captain's
face.

'Because it's of no use,' cried Rolph.   'I've tried
till I'm sick of trying.   I want to tell you.'

'Oh, but you mustn't tell me,' said Lucy.

'Oh, yes I must, and I'm going to begin now.   I
shall tell you all my ventures, and what I win, and
when I am going to train; and—I say, Lucy, you did
come out this morning to see me train?'

'Indeed, I did not,' she cried; 'and even if I had,
I should not tell you so.'

'Oh, I don't mind,' said Rolph, laughing.   'I'm
satisfied.'

'What a monster for poor Glynne to be engaged
to.   I believe, if I were to encourage him, he'd break
off his engagement.'

'I am glad I met you,' said Rolph, suddenly, and
he went a little closer to Lucy, who started aside into
the wet grass, and glanced hastily round.   'Why, what
are you doing?' he said.

'I wanted to pick that mushroom,' she said.

'Oh, never mind the mushrooms, you'll make your little feet wet, and I want to talk to you. I say, I'm going to train again to-morrow morning. You'll come, won't you. Pray do!— Who's this?'

Both started, for, having approached unheard, his pony's paces muffled by the turf, Philip Oldroyd cantered by them, gazing hard at Lucy, and raising his hat stiffly to Rolph, as he went past.

'Confound him! Where did he spring from?' cried Rolph. 'Why, he quite startled you,' he continued, for Lucy's face, which had flushed crimson, now turned of a pale waxen hue.

'Oh, no; it is nothing,' she said, as a tremor ran through her frame, and she hesitated as to what she should do, ending by exclaiming suddenly that she must go back home at once.

'But you'll come and see me train to-morrow morning,' said Rolph.

'No, no. Oh, no. I could not,' cried Lucy; and she turned and hurried away.

'But you will come,' said Rolph, gazing after her. 'I'll lay two to one—five to one—fifty to one—she comes. She's caught—wired—netted. Pretty little rustic-looking thing. I rather like the little lassie; she's so fresh and innocent. I wonder what dignified Madame Glynne would say. Bet a hundred to one little Lucy's thinking about me now, and making up her mind to come.'

He was right; Lucy was thinking about him, and wishing he had been at the bottom of the sea that morning before he had met her.

'Oh, what will Mr Oldroyd think?' she sobbed, as the tears ran down her face. 'It's nothing to him, and he's nothing to me; but it's horrible for him to have seen me walking out at this time in the morning, and *alone*, with that stupid, common, racing, betting creature, whom I absolutely abominate.'

She walked on, weeping silently for a few minutes before resuming her self-reproaches.

'I'm afraid it was very wicked and wrong and forward of me, but I did so want to know whether he really cared for Glynne. And he doesn't—he doesn't —he does not,' she sobbed passionately. 'He's a wicked, bad, empty-headed, deceitful monster; and he'd make Glynne wretched all her life. Why, he was making love to me, and talking slightingly of her all the time.'

Here there was another burst of sobs, in the midst of which, and the accompanying blinding tears, she stooped down to pick another mushroom, but only to viciously throw it away, for it to fall bottom upwards impaled upon the sharp thorns of a green furze bush close at hand.

'I don't care,' she cried; 'they may think what they like, both of them, and they may say what they like. I was trying to fight my poor, dear, injured, darling brother's battle, and to make things happier for him, and if I'm a martyr through it, I will be, and I don't care a pin.'

She was walking on, blinded by the veil of tears that fell from her eyes, seeing nothing, hearing nothing of the song of birds and the whirr and hum of the insect world. The morning was now glorious, and the wild, desolate common land was full of beauty; but Lucy's heart was sore with trouble, and outburst followed outburst as she went homeward.

'I've found him out, though, after all, and it's worth every pain I may feel, and Glynne shall know what a wretch he is, and then she'll turn to poor, dear Moray, and he'll be happy once again. Poor fellow, how he has suffered, and without a word, believing that there was no hope for him when there is; and I don't care, I'm growing reckless now; I'd even let Glynne see how unworthy Captain Rolph is, by going to meet him. It doesn't matter a bit, people will believe I'm weak and silly; and if the captain were to boast that he had won me, everybody would believe him. Oh, it's dreadful, dreadful, I want to do mischief to some one else and—and—and—but I don't care, not a bit. Yes, I do,' she sobbed bitterly. 'Everybody will think me a weak, foolish, untrustworthy girl, and it will break my heart, and—oh!'

Lucy stopped short, tear-blinded, having nearly run against an obstacle in the way.

The obstacle was Lucy's mental definition of 'everybody,' who would think slightingly of her now.

For 'everybody' was seated upon a pony, waiting evidently for her to come.

CHAPTER VII.

STARLIGHT DOINGS.

IT was astonishing how great the interest in the stars had now become in the neighbourhood of Brackley. Glynne was studying hard so as to learn something of the wondrous orbs of whose astounding nature Moray Alleyne loved to speak; and now Philip Oldroyd had told himself that it would be far better if he were not quite so ignorant on matters astronomical.

The result was that he had purchased a book or two giving accounts of the Royal Observatory, the peculiarities of the different instruments used, the various objects most studied; and in these works he was coaching himself up as fast as he could on the present night—having 'a comfortable read' as he called it, before going to bed—when there came a bit of a novelty for him, a sudden summons to go and see a patient.

'What's the matter?' he said, going to the door to answer the call, after a glance at his watch, to see that it was half-past twelve.

'Well, sir,' said the messenger, Caleb Kent, 'it's mate o' mine hurt hissen like, somehow. Met of a fall, I think.'

'Fall, eh? Where is he hurt?'

'Mostlings 'bout the 'ead, sir, but he's a bit touched all over.'

'What did he fall off—a cart?'

'No, sir, it warn't off a cart. Hadn't you better come and see him, sir?'

'Of course, my man, but I don't want to go away from home, and then find I might have taken something, and saved my patient a great deal of suffering.'

'Yes, sir; quite right, sir,' said the man mysteriously; 'well, you see, sir, I can't talk about it like. It weer a fall certainly, but some one made him fall.'

'Oh, a fight, eh?'

'Yes, sir; there was a bit of a fight.'

'Well, if your mate has been fighting, is he bad enough to want a doctor?'

'He's down bad, sir. It warn't fisties.'

'Sticks?'

The man nodded.

'Anything worse?'

'Well, sir, I didn't mean to speak about it, but it weer.'

'I think I have it,' thought Oldroyd. 'The man has been shot in a poaching affray. Where is it?' he said aloud.

Lars cottage through Lindham, sir. Tile roof.'

'Six miles away?'

'Yes, sir; 'bout six miles.'

As Oldroyd spoke, he was busily thrusting a case or two and some lint into his pockets, and filling a couple of small phials; after which he buttoned up his coat and put out his lamp.

'Now, then, my man, I must just call at the mill, and then I'm ready for you.'

'Going to walk, sir?' said the messenger.

'No; I'm going to. get the miller's pony. I'm sorry I can't offer to drive you back.'

'Never you mind about me, sir. I can get over the ground,' said the man; and following Oldroyd down the lane, he stopped with him at a long low cottage, close beside the dammed up river, where a couple of sharp raps caused a casement to be opened.

'You, doctor?' said a voice; and on receiving an answer in the affirmative, there was the word 'catch,' and Oldroyd cleverly caught a key attached by a string to a very large horse-chestnut. Then the casement was closed, and the two went round to the stable, where a stout pony's slumbers were interrupted, and the patient beast saddled and bridled and led out, ready to spread its four legs as far apart as possible when the young doctor mounted as if afraid of being pulled over by his weight.

'Now, then,' said Oldroyd, relocking the door,

'forward as fast as you like. When you're tired I'll get down.'

'Oh, I sha'n't be tired,' said the man, quietly; and he started off at a regular dog-trot. 'That there pony'll go anywhere, sir, so I shall take the short cuts.'

'Mind the boggy bits, my man.'

'You needn't be skeard about them, sir; that there pony wouldn't near one if you tried to make him.'

Oldroyd nodded, and the man trotted to the front, the pony following, and, in spite of two or three proposals that they should change places, the guide kept on in the same untiring manner.

Here and there, though, when they had passed the common, and were ascending the hills, the man took hold of the pony's mane, and trudged by the side; and during these times Oldroyd learned all about the fight in the fir-wood.

'Whose place was it at?' said Oldroyd at last.

'Sir John Day's, sir.'

After that they proceeded in silence till they reached the first houses of a long, straggling hamlet, when a thought occurred to Oldroyd to which he at once gave utterance.

'I say, my man, why didn't you go to Doctor Blunt? He was two miles nearer to you than I am.'

Caleb laughed hoarsely, and shook his head.

Oldroyd checked his willing little mount at a long,

low cottage beside the road, and went down the strip of garden. Three men were at the door, and they made way for him, touching their hats in a surly fashion as he came up.

'Know how he is?' said Oldroyd, sharply.

''Bout gone, sir. Glad you've come,' said one of the men; and Oldroyd raised the latch and went into the low-ceiled kitchen, where a tallow candle was burning in a lantern, but there was no one there.

'Here's the doctor, miss,' said the man who had before spoken, crossing to a doorway opening at once upon a staircase, when a frightened-looking girl, with red eyes and a scared look upon her countenance, came hurrying downstairs.

'Would you please to come up, sir,' she said. 'Oh, I am so glad you've come.'

Oldroyd followed her up the creaking staircase, and had to stoop to enter the sloping-ceiled room, where, with another pale, scared woman kneeling beside the bed, and a long, snuffed candle upon an old chest of drawers, giving a doleful, ghastly light, lay a big, black-whiskered, shaggy-haired man, his face pinched and white, and plenty of tokens about of the terrible wound he had received.

Oldroyd went at once to the bed, made a hurried examination, took out his case, and for the next half hour he was busy trying to staunch the bleeding, and place some effectual bandages upon the wound.

All this time the man never opened his eyes, but lay with his teeth clenched, and lips nipped so closely together, that they seemed to form a thin line across the lower part of his face. Oldroyd knew that he must be giving the man terrible pain, but he did not shrink, bearing it all stoically, if he was conscious, though there were times when his attendant thought he must be perfectly insensible to what was going on.

The women obeyed the slightest hint, and worked hard ; but all the while Oldroyd felt that he had been called upon too late, and that the man must sink from utter exhaustion.

To his surprise, however, just as he finished his task, and was bending over his patient counting the pulsation in the wrist, the man unclosed his eyes, and looked up at him.

'Well, doctor,' he said, coolly ; 'what's it to be—go or stay?'

'Life, I hope,' replied Oldroyd, as he read the energy and determination of the man's nature. This was not one who would give up without a struggle, for his bearing during the past half hour had been heroic.

'Glad of it,' sighed the wounded man. 'I haven't done yet ; and to-night's work has given me a fresh job on hand.'

'Now, keep perfectly still and do not speak,' said Oldroyd, sternly. 'Everything depends upon your being at rest. Sleep if you can. I will stop till morning to see that the bleeding does not break out again.'

'Thankye, doctor,' said the man gruffly ; and just then a pair of warm lips were pressed upon Oldroyd's hand, and he turned sharply.

'Hallo!' he said. 'I've been so busy that I did not notice you. I've seen your face before.'

'Yes, sir ; I met you once near The Warren—Mrs Rolph's.'

'Thought I'd seen you. But you—are you his wife?'

'No,' said the girl, smiling faintly. 'This is my father.'

'What an absurd blunder. Why, of course, I re-member now. I did not know him again. It's Mrs Rolph's keeper.

The flush that came into the girl's face was visible even by the faint light of the miserable tallow candle, as Oldroyd went on in a low voice,—

'Poor fellow! I misjudged him. I took him for a poacher, and its the other way on. The scoundrels ! No, no, don't give way,' whispered Oldroyd, as the girl let her face fall into her hands and began to sob convulsively. 'There, there : cheer up. We won't let him die. You and I will pull him through, please God. Hush! quietness is everything. Go and tell those men to be still, and say I shall not want the pony till six or seven o'clock. One of them must be ready, though, in case I want a messenger to run to the town.'

Oldroyd's words had their effect, for a dead silence fell upon the place, and the injured man soon slept quietly, lying so still, that Judith, after her return, sought the young doctor's eyes from time to time, asking dumbly whether he was sure that something terrible had not occurred.

At such times Oldroyd rose, bent over his patient and satisfied himself that all was going well before turning to his fellow-watcher and giving her an encouraging smile.

Then there would be a weary sigh, that told of relief from an anxiety full of dread, and the night wore on.

For a time, Oldroyd, as he sat there in that dreary room, glancing occasionally at the dull, unsnuffed candle, fancied that the men had stolen away, but he would soon know that he was wrong, for the faint odour of their bad tobacco came stealing up through the window, and he knew as well as if he were present that they were sitting about on the fence or lounging against the walls of the cottage.

Between three and four, the critical time of the twenty-four hours, when life is at its lowest ebb, a sigh came from the bed, and the sufferer grew restless to a degree that made Oldroyd begin to be doubtful, but the little uneasy fit passed off, and there was utter silence once again.

Philip Oldroyd's thoughts wandered far during this time of watching ; now his imagination raised for his mental gaze the scene of the desperate encounter, and he seemed to see the blows struck, hear the oaths and fierce cries, succeeded by the report of the gun, and the groan of the injured man as he fell.

Then that scene seemed to pass away, and the room at The Firs came into sight, with its grim, blank look, the stiff figure of Mrs Alleyne ; calm, deeply absorbed Alleyne ; and the sunshine of the whole place, Lucy, who seemed to turn what was blank and repulsive into all that was bright and gay.

As he thought on of Lucy all the gloom and ghastliness of that wretched cottage garret faded away, a pleasant glow of satisfaction came over him, and he sat there building dreamy castles of a bright and prosperous kind, and putting Lucy in each, forgetting for the time the poverty of his practice, his own comparatively hopeless state, and the chances that she, whom he now owned that he worshipped, would be carried off by some one more successful in the world.

Did he love Lucy ? Yes, he told himself, he was afraid he did—afraid, for it seemed so hopeless an affair. Did she love him ? No, he dared not think that, but at one time, during the most weary portion of the watching, he could not help wishing that she might fall ill, and the duty be his to bring her back to health and strength.

He was angry with himself directly after, though
he owned that such a trouble might fill her with
gratitude towards him, and gratitude was a step
towards love.

In the midst of these thoughts Oldroyd made himself more angry still, for he inadvertently sighed, with
the effect of making the women start, and Judith
gaze at him wonderingly. To take off their attention
he softly shifted his seat, and began once more to
think of his patient and his chances of life.

The poor fellow was sleeping easily, and so far
there were no signs of the feverish symptoms that
follow wounds.

The night wore on ; the candle burned down in the
socket, and was replaced by another, which in its turn
burned out, and its successor was growing short
when the twitterings of the birds were heard, and the
ghostly dawn came stealing into that cheerless, white-
washed room, whose occupants' faces seemed to have
taken their hue from the ceiling.

The injured man still slept, and his breathing was
low and regular, encouraged by which the counten-
ances of the women were beginning to lose their despairing, scared aspect, as they glanced from doctor
to patient, and back again.

At last the cold and pallid light of the room gave
place to a warm red glow, and Oldroyd went softly to
the window to see the rising sun, thinking the while
what a dreary life was his, called from his comfort-

able home to come some six miles in the dead of the night to such a ghastly scene as this, and then to sit and watch, his payment probably the thanks of the poor people he had served.

The east was one glow of orange and gold, and the beauty of the scene, with the dewy grass and trees glittering in the morning light, chased away the mental shadows of the night.

'Not so bad a life after all,' he said to himself. 'Money's very nice, but a man can't devote his life to greed. What a glorious morning, and how I should like a cup of tea.'

He turned to look at his patient, and found that the woman had gone, while Judith now asked him in an imploring whisper if there was any hope.'

'Hope? Yes,' he replied, 'it would have killed some men, but look at your father's physique. Why, he is as strong as a horse. Take care of him and keep him quiet. Let him sleep all he can.'

Judith glanced at the wounded man, and then at Oldroyd, to whisper at last piteously, and after a good deal of hesitation,—

'The police, sir: if they come, they mustn't take him away, must they?'

'Take him away?' said Oldroyd, wonderingly, 'certainly not. I say he must not be moved. Here, I'll write it down for you. It would be his death.'

He drew out his pocket-book to write a certificate as to the man's state, and Judith took it, with an air approaching veneration, to fold it and place it in her bosom.

Just then the woman returned, and, after a whispering with Judith, asked Oldroyd to come down.

He glanced once more at his patient, and then followed the girl downstairs, where, in a rough but cleanly way, a cup of tea had been prepared and some bread and butter.

These proved to be so good that, feeling better for the refreshment, Oldroyd could not help noticing that, but for the traces of violent grief, Judith would have been extremely pretty.

'Will father get better, sir?' said the girl, pleadingly.

'Better? Yes, my girl,' said Oldroyd, wondering at the rustic maiden's good looks. 'There, there, don't be foolish,' he continued, as the girl caught his hand to kiss it.

She shrank away, and coloured a little, when Oldroyd hastened to add more pleasantly,—

'I think he'll soon be better.'

She gave him a bright, grateful look through her tears, and then hurriedly shrank away.

'Hah! that's better,' he said to himself, as he went on with his simple meal. 'A cup of tea, and a little sunshine, what a difference they do make in a man's sensations. Humph! past six. No bed for me till to-night,' he exclaimed, as he glanced at his watch; and rising, he went softly upstairs once more, to find that his patient was still sleeping, with Judith watching by his pillow.

Oldroyd just nodded to her, and made a motion with one finger that she should come to his side.

' I'll ride over in the afternoon,' he whispered ; and then he went quietly down, said 'good-morning' to the woman waiting, and with the sensation upon him that the night's work did not seem so horrible now that the sun had risen, he stepped out.

CHAPTER VIII.

WHY THE SLUGS ATE LUCY'S MUSHROOMS.

THREE men, one of whom was the last night's messenger, Caleb Kent, a stranger to Oldroyd, were lounging about by the cottage gate as the doctor stepped out, and their looks asked the question they longed to have answered.

'I think he'll get over it, my men,' said Oldroyd. 'It's a narrow escape for him, though, if he does pull through.'

The men exchanged glances.

'I suppose you'll have the police over before long, and— What's the matter?'

The men were looking sharply down the road.

'I mean they'll want to question him about the scoundrels who did this work.'

'It warn't no scoundrels, did it, doctor,' said Caleb Kent, with a vicious snarl.

'But I took it that the keeper had been shot by poachers.'

'It were Cap'n Rolph shot him,' said Caleb, fiercely.

'Dear me! What a sad accident.'

'Accident?' cried Caleb Kent, with an ugly laugh. 'Why, I see him lift his gun and take aim. It was just as I was going to hit at him.'

'Nonsense, my lad : his own master.'

'Arn't no master of his'n now. Sacked nigh three months ago.'

Oldroyd stared.

'Here, I'm getting confused, my man. That poor fellow upstairs is a keeper, isn't he?'

'Was, sir,' said Caleb Kent, with a grin; 'but he arn't now. He was out with us after the fezzans last night.'

'Hold your tongue,' growled one of the other men.

'Sha'n't. What for? Doctor won't tell on us.'

'Then it is as I thought. You are a gang of poachers, and the man upstairs is hand and glove with you.'

'Well, why not, sir. They sacked him, and no one wouldn't have him, because he used once to do a bit o' nights hisself 'fore he turned keeper. Man can't starve when there's hares and fezzans about.'

'Went a bit like out o' spite,' said Caleb. 'Hadn't been out with us before.'

'Humph! and you come and fetch me and tell me this,' said Oldroyd. 'How do you know that I shall not go and give notice to the police?'

''Cause we know'd better. Caleb here was going to fetch old Blunt from the town; but I says if you fetch him, he'll go back and tell the police.'

'And how do you know that I shall not?' said Oldroyd, tartly.

'Gent as goes out of his way to tent a poor labrer's wife when her chap's out o' work, and does so much for the old folks, arn't likely to do such a dirty trick as that. Eh, mates?'

'Humph! you seem to have a pretty good opinion of me,' said Oldroyd.

'Yes, sir, we knows a gen'leman when we sees one. We'll pay you, sir, all right. You won't let out on us, seeing how bad the poor fellow is.'

Oldroyd was silent and thoughtful for a few moments, and then he turned sharply upon Caleb Kent.

'Look here, sir,' he said; 'you've got a tongue and it runs rather too fast. You made an ugly charge against that man's late master.'

'I said I see him shute him,' said Caleb.

'And you did not see anything of the kind.'

'You gents allus stick up for each other,' muttered Caleb.

'You could not see what took place in the darkness and excitement of a fight, so hold your tongue. Such a charge would make endless mischief, and it must be a mistake.'

'All right, sir,' said Caleb.

'It would upset that poor girl, too, if she heard such a thing.'

'Yes, it would upset her sure enough if she heard,'

said Caleb, with a peculiar smile, and he walked away.

'I ought to give you fellows a lecture on the danger of night poaching,' continued Oldroyd.

'Don't, sir, please,' said one of the men, with a laugh, 'for it wouldn't do no good. 'Sides; we might want to hing a brace o' fezzans or a hare up agin your door now and then.'

'Here, don't you do anything of the kind, my lads,' cried Oldroyd. 'I forbid it, mind. Now get me my pony.'

'All right, sir; we'll mind what you says,' said the man who had spoken, looking mirthfully round at his companions, one of whom at once accompanied him to a low shed where the pony was munching some hay. The willing little beast was saddled while Oldroyd walked up and down the path with an abundance of sweet-scented and gay old-fashioned flowers on either side. Carnations and scarlet lychnis, and many-headed sun flowers and the like, were bright in the morning sunshine, for all seemed to have been well tended; but, all at once, he came upon a terrible tell-tale bit of evidence of the last night's work upon the red bricks that formed the path—one that made him scrape off a little mould from the bed with his foot, and spread it over the ugly patch.

'The cottage looks simple and innocent enough, with its roses, to be the home of peace,' he muttered. 'Ah! how man does spoil his life for the sake of coin.

Thank you, my lad—that's right,' he added, as his last night's messenger brought the pony to the gate.

He mounted, and thrust a coin, that he could not spare, into his temporary ostler's hand.

'Let him go.   Fine morning, isn't it?'

But Caleb held on sturdily by the pony's bridle, and thrust the piece back with an air of sturdy independence.

'No, thankye, sir,' he said.   'Me and my mates don't want paying by a gentleman as comes to help one of us.   'Sides which, we're a-going to pay you; arn't we, lads?'

'Ay, that's so,' growled the others.   'Don't take it.'

With the cleverness of a pickpocket, but the reverse action—say of a negative and not a positive pickpocket—the florin was thrust into Oldroyd's vest, and the man drew back, leaving the doctor to pursue his way.

'Poachers even are not so black as they are painted,' he said to himself as he cantered along, and then he fell to thinking of the girl he had seen that morning. 'They've better daughters than you would have suspected, more affectionate wives, the best of neighbours, and companions as honest and faithful as one could wish; and, all the while, they are a set of confounded scoundrels and thieves, for it's just as dishonest to shoot and steal a man's carefully-raised foreign birds—his pheasants—as it is to break into a hen-roost.   As to partridges and hares, of course they are wild things; but, so long as they lived and bred on one's land, they must be as genuine property as the apples and pears that grow upon a fellow's trees. Yes, poachers are thieves; and I daresay my friend there, with the shot-hole in his body, is as great a scoundrel as the worst.'

He laughed as he cantered along the soft green beside the road.

'My practice is improving. I shall have my connection amongst the rogues and vagabonds mightily increased, for I certainly shall not go and inform the police: not my business to do that. They're punished enough, even if I pull him through. And I shall,' he said aloud. 'I must and will, for the sake of his pretty daughter. I wonder whether they'll pay me after all,' he went on, as the pony ambled over the grass, and the naturally sordid ideas of the man often pressed for money and struggling for his income, came uppermost. 'When people are in the first throes of excitement and gratitude for the help Doctor Bolus has rendered them, they almost worship him, and they'll give, or rather they will promise, anything; but when time has had his turn, and the gratitude has begun to cool, it's a different thing altogether; and, last of all, when the bill goes in — oh dear, for poor human nature, if the case had been left alone, A, B, C, or D would have got better without help.

'Well, never mind,' he said merrily, for the refreshment and the delicious morning air were telling upon his spirits, 'the world goes round and round all the same, and human nature is one of the things that cannot be changed.'

He had to turn the pony out on to the road here, for the long green strands of the brambles were hanging right out over the grass, and catching at his legs as he cantered by. The soft mists were floating away as he began to descend the hilly slope, still at his feet the landscape seemed to be half hidden by clouds, through which hillocks, and hedge, and trees were visible, with here and there a house or a brown patch of the rough common land ; and right away on the other side, stood up, grim and depressing of aspect, the ugly brick house upon the big hillock of sand, with the various and grim-looking edifices that Moray Alleyne had raised. Forming a background were the sombre fir trees with the column-topped slope and hill ; and, even at that distance, he could make out, here and there, portions of the sandy lane that skirted the pine slope, which formed so striking an object in the surrounding landscape.

So beautiful was the scene in the early morning, so varied the tints, that Oldroyd checked his pony, and told himself that he could not do better than pause and admire the landscape. But somehow his eyes lit upon the ugliest object there, focused themselves so as to get the most photographic idea upon the polished plate of his memory, and there they stayed, for he saw nothing else but Mrs Alleyne's gloomy house.

This, however, is not quite the fact, for in a most absurd way—for a young medical man who had been telling himself a hundred times over that it would be insanity for him to think of marrying—he furnished that gloomy picture with one figure that seemed to him to turn the whole place into a palace of beauty, of whose aspect he could never tire.

'Go along!' he exclaimed aloud at last, as if to himself for his absurd thoughts; but the pony took the order as being applied to the beast of burden present, and went off at once in a good canter, one that gained spirit from the fact that he knew the way and that way was homewards.

So absorbed was Oldroyd that he left the sturdy little animal to itself, and it went pretty swiftly over the driest bits of close, velvety turf, cleverly avoiding the bigger furze clumps, and reaching at last the lighter ground where the fir trees grew. Then it snorted and would have increased its pace, but there were awkward stumps here and there, and slippery places, such as the cleverest pony could not avoid, so the rider drew rein, and let the little steed amble gently along.

All at once Philip Oldroyd's heart seemed to stand still, and he checked the pony suddenly, sitting breathless and half stunned, gazing straight before him at a couple of figures passing along the road.

He drew a long breath that hissed between his

closed teeth; and even a pearl diver might have envied his power of retaining that breath, so long was it before he exhaled it again.

Then he turned his pony's head, bent down his darkened face till his chin rested upon his breast, and rode forward again; but the pony began to resist a change which suggested going right away from home. He drummed its ribs fiercely with his heels, and pressed it on, but only to turn its head directly after, forcing himself into a state of composure as he rode quietly by Lucy Alleyne and Rolph, and saluted them as he passed.

It was hard work to ride on like that, without looking back, but he mastered himself and went quickly on for some distance before drawing rein, and sitting like a statue upon the pony, which began to graze, and only lifted its head and gave a momentary glance at Lucy, when, sobbing as if she would break her heart, the little lady nearly ran up against the waiting rider and his steed.

'Mr Oldroyd!' cried Lucy, after giving vent to that astonished, frightened 'Oh!'

'Yes, Miss Alleyne,' he said coldly, 'Mr Oldroyd.'

'Why—why are you stopping me like that? Oh, I beg your pardon; good-morning!' she cried hastily, and in a quick, furtive way she swept the tears from her eyes, and wiped her pretty little nose, which crying was turning of a pinky hue.

'Was I stopping you?' he said, speaking mechanic-

ally, and glancing straight before him. ' I have been
out all night with a patient six miles away.'

' Indeed !' said Lucy, hastily ; 'yes, it is a beautiful
morning.'

She went by him without trusting herself to look
in his face.

' If I did so, I should burst out sobbing,' she said to
herself.

But by the time Lucy had gone half a score
yards, Oldroyd was by her side, the pony keeping
step with her, pace for pace, while the little woman's
breast was heaving with love, sorrow and despair.

' What will he think ? what will he think ? ' she kept
saying to herself as she longed to lay her hands in his,
and to tell him that it was no fault of hers, but an accident that Captain Rolph had met her during her walk.

But she could not tell him—she dared not. It
was like a confession that she cared for his opinion
more than for that of anybody in the world. It would
be unmaidenly, and degrading, and strange ; and
there was nothing for her to do but assume anger
and annoyance, and treat Oldroyd as if he had been
playing the part of spy.

A very weak conclusion, no doubt, but it was the
only one at which, in her misery, she arrived.

The sun was shining now from a pure, blue sky, the
birds were darting beneath the trees, where the long
spider webs hung, strung with jewels, that flashed
and glowed as they were passing fast away. There

was a delicious aroma, too, in the soft breeze that
floated from among the gloomy pines ; but to those
who went on, side by side, it was as if the morning
had become overcast ; all was stormy and grey, and
life was in future to be one long course of desolation
and despair.   Nature was at her best, and all was
beautiful ; but Lucy could not see a ray of hope in the
far-off future.   Philip Oldroyd could see a gloomy,
wasted life—the life of a man who had trusted and
believed ; but to find that the woman was weak and
vain as the rest of her sex.

They had relapsed into silence, and were going on
pretty swiftly towards The Firs, but their proceedings
did not seem to either to be at all strange.   Lucy's
destination was, of course, home, and Oldroyd appeared resolved to accompany her ; why, he knew not,
and it did not trouble him after the first few minutes,
seeming quite natural that he should take her to
task, and he determined, as a punishment, to see her
safely back.   She did not deserve it, of that she was
sure, but there was something comfortable and satis-
factory in being thus silently scolded by one much
wiser and stronger than herself.

Oldroyd wished to speak.   He had a good deal to
say—so he felt, but not a word escaped him till they
reached the steep path that ran up to the gates at The
Firs, when he drew rein, and made way for Lucy to
pass.

'Good-bye,' he said.

'Good-bye,' faltered Lucy, looking at him wistfully.

He looked down into her eyes from where he sat, with his very heart ready to leap from his breast towards her; but, as he gazed, he saw again the sunny sandy road with the velvety grass, and golden-bloomed furze on either side; the long, sloping bank with its columnar pines, and the dark background of sombre green, while in front was Lucy, the girl in whom he had so believed, walking with Rolph; and then all was bitterness and cloud once more.

'He was marked,' thought Oldroyd; 'there was a patch of plaister on his forehead. Hang it all! could he have shot that man?'

The doctor's heart beat fast, for, in a confused fashion, light, the glimmering light upon a reflector when an image plays about the focus of a telescope, he saw difficulties dragging Captain Rolph away from that neighbourhood: a man dying of his wounds, and Lucy Alleyne turning from her idol in utter disgust.

But he shook his head.

'Nothing to me,' he cried, with a bitter laugh, as he rode away. 'The old story—Nature asserting herself once more. A fine figure, grand muscles, a chest that is deep and round, and the noble bovine front of a bull, and you have the demi-god gentle woman makes her worship. Ah, well, it was time I awakened from a silly dream. Good-bye, little Lucy, good-bye!

Next time I come to see your brother, I'll wear the armoured jerkin of common sense. What a weak idiot I have been.'

There were no mushrooms that morning for Mrs Alleyne's breakfast; those which Lucy should have brought home lying by the wayside, whereat the slugs rejoiced and had a glorious banquet all to themselves.

CHAPTER IX.

THE MAJOR HAPPENS TO BE THERE.

A POACHING affray was too common an affair in the neighbourhood of Brackley to make much stir. Sir John went in for two or three discussions with his keepers, and the rural policeman had been summoned, this worthy feeling sure that he would be able—in his own words—to put his hand upon the parties; but though the officer might have had the ability to put his hand upon the parties, he did not do so, or if he did, he forgot to close it. Then the dog was buried, and as a set off, Sir John had a fire made of the nets and stakes that had been taken from the gang; these, and their spoil of several brace of pheasants and partridges and a few hares, having been left behind in their hurried flight.

So, as it happened, the active and intelligent constable made no discoveries; but Rolph did, and whereas the one would have revelled in the hopes of promotion, and in seeing his name several times in the county paper; the other, when he had made his discovery, said only—and to himself—that it was ' doosid awkward,' and held his peace.

'I never did see such a girl as you are to read,' said Rolph, entering the drawing-room one after-noon, when he had ridden over from Aldershot; 'at it again.'

He spoke lightly and merrily, and Glynne hastily put aside her book, and rose from her chair.

'Did you want me to go out for a ride, Robert?' she said rather eagerly.

'Well, no; not this afternoon.'

The smile Glynne had called up, and which came with an unbidden flush, died out slowly, and a look of calmness, even of relief, dawned upon her coun-tenance as the young man went on.

'Thought you wouldn't mind if we didn't go this afternoon. Looks a bit doubtful, too. Quite fine, now, but the weather does change so rapidly.'

'Does it?' said Glynne, looking at him rather wistfully.

'Yes. I think it's the pine woods. High trees. Attract moisture. Don't say it is, dear. I'm not big at that sort of thing, but we do have a deal of rain here.'

'Why, papa was complaining the other day about want of water,' said Glynne, smiling

'Ah, that was for his turnips. They want rain You won't be disappointed?'

'I?—oh, no,' said Glynne, quietly.

'Think I'll do a bit of training this afternoon. I'm not quite up to the mark.'

'Are you always going to train so much, dear?' said Glynne, thoughtfully.

'Always? Eh? Always? Oh, no; of course not ; but it's a man's duty to get himself up to the very highest pitch of health and strength. But if you'd set your mind upon a ride, we'll go.'

'I?—oh, no,' said Glynne. 'I thought you wished it, dear.'

'That's all right then,' said Rolph, cheerfully. 'By-bye, beauty,' he said, kissing her. 'I say, Glynne, 'pon my word, I think you are the most lovely woman I ever saw.'

She smiled at him as he turned at the doorway, nodding back at her, and she remained fixed to the spot as the captain, cigar in mouth, passed directly after, turning to kiss his hand as he saw her dimly through the window.

For Glynne did not run across the room to stand and watch him till he was out of sight, but remained where he had left her, with a couple of dull red spots glowing in her cheeks for a time, and then dying slowly out, leaving her very pale.

Glynne was thinking deeply, and it was evident that her thoughts were giving her pain, for her eyes darkened, then half-closed, and she slowly walked up and down the room a few times, and then returned to her chair, to bend over, rest her head upon her hand, and sit gazing straight before her at the soft carpet, remaining almost motionless for quite half-an-hour, when she sighed deeply, took up her book, and continued reading.

Rolph went right off at once through the park and out across the long meadow and into the fir wood, where, as if led by some feeling of attraction, he made for the spot where the encounter had taken place a week before, and stopped for a few minutes to gaze at the ground, as if he expected to see the traces still there.

'Tchah! he exclaimed, impatiently; 'it was an accident. Guns will go off sometimes.'

He wrenched himself away, walking on amongst the trees rapidly for a time, and then stopped to relight his cigar, whose near end was a good deal gnawed and shortened.

'Tchah!' he ejaculated again. 'I won't think of it. Just as well blame oneself, if a fellow in one's troop goes down, and breaks his leg in a charge.'

He puffed furiously at his cigar as he went on, and then forgot it again, so that it went out, and he threw it away impatiently, thrust his hands into his pockets, and walked as fast as the nature of the ground would permit.

For, evidently with the idea of giving himself a very severe course of training, he kept in the woods where the pathways were rugged and winding and so little frequented that at times the young growth crossed, switching his hat or face, and often having to be beaten back by the hands which he unwillingly withdrew from his pockets.

Rolph probably meant to reach some particular spot before he turned, for twice over he crossed a lane, and instead of taking advantage of the better path afforded, he plunged again into the woods and went on.

At the end of an hour he came upon another lane more solitary and unused than those he had passed. It was a mere track occasionally used by the wood-cutters for a timber wagon, and the marks of the broad wheels were here and there visible in the white sand, which as a rule trickled down into all depressions, fine as that in an hour-glass, and hid the marks left by man.

'Rather warm,' muttered Rolph as he was crossing the sandy track ; and he was in the act of charging up the bank on the other side, when there was a cheery hail, and as he turned with an angry ejaculation, he became aware of the fact that Sir John was coming along the lane upon one of his ponies, whose tread was unheard in the soft sand.

'Why, hullo, Rob, where are you going?' cried the baronet. 'You look like a lost man in a forest.'

'Do I? oh, only having a good breather. Getting a little too much fat. Must keep myself down. Ride very heavy with all my accoutrements.'

'Hah! Yes. You're a big fellow,' said Sir John, looking at him rather fixedly. 'Why didn't you

have the horses out, then, and take Glynne for a
ride?'

'Glynne? By Jove, sir, I did propose it, only she
had got a book in the drawing-room.'

'D—n the books ' cried Sir John, pettishly. ' She
reads too much. But, hang it all, Rob, my lad, don't
let her grow into a book-worm because she's engaged.
She's not half the girl she was before this fixture, as
you'd call it, was made.'

' Well, really, I—'

' Yes, yes, I know what you'd say. You do your
best. But, hang it all, don't let her mope, and be
always indoors. Plenty of time for that when there
are half-a-dozen children in the nursery, eh? Coming back my way?'

'No. Oh, no,' cried Rolph, hastily; ' I must finish
my walk. I shall take a short cut back. Been for a
ride?'

'I? Pooh! I don't go for rides, my lad. I've
been to see my sheep on the hills, and I've another
lot to see. There, good-bye till dinner-time, if you
won't come.'

He touched his pony's ribs and cantered off. Rolph
plunging into the wood, and hastily glancing at his
watch as he hurried on.

' Lovers are different to what they were when I was
a young fellow,' said Sir John. ' We were a bit
chivalrous and attentive then. Pooh! So they are
now. There's no harm in the lad. It isn't such a

bad thing to keep his body in a state of perfection—
real perfection of health and strength. Makes a young
fellow moral and pure-minded; but I wish he would
devote himself more to Glynne. Take her out more;
she looks too pale.'

'Hang him! I wish he had been at Jericho,'
muttered the subject of Sir John's thoughts. 'Let's
see, I can keep along all the way in the woods now.
I sha'n't meet any one there.'

The prophecy concerning people held good
for a quarter of an hour or so, and then, turning rapidly into an open fir glade, Rolph found
out that being prophetic does not pay without a
long preliminary preparation, and an ingenious
consideration of probabilities and the like, for
he suddenly came plump upon the major, stoop-
ing down, trowel in hand—so suddenly, in fact,
that he nearly fell over him, and the two started
back, the one with a muttered oath, the other with
words of surprise.

'Why, I didn't expect to find you in this out-of-
the-way place,' said the major.

'By Jove, that's just what I was going to say,' cried
Rolph.

'Not raw beef-steaks this time, is it?' said the
major with a grim look full of contempt.

'Steaks—raw steaks. I don't understand you.'

'This is rough woodland; you are not training now,
are you?' said the major, carefully placing what

looked like a handful of dirty little blackish potatoes in his fishing creel.

'Training? Well, yes, of course I am. Keeping myself up to the mark,' retorted Rolph. 'A soldier, in my opinion, ought to be the very perfection of manly strength.'

'Well, yes,' said the major, rubbing the soil off one of his dirty little truffles, and then polishing his bright little steel trowel with a piece of newspaper, 'but the men of my time did pretty well with no other training than their military drill.'

'*Autres*—I forget the rest,' said Rolph. 'I never was good at French. It means other fellows had other manners in other times, major. Got a good haul of toadstools?'

'No, sir, I have not got a good haul of toadstools to-day; but I have unearthed a few truffles. Should you like a dish for dinner?'

'Thanks, no. Not coming my way, I suppose?'

'No,' said the major. 'I think I shall trudge back.'

'Ho!' exclaimed Rolph. 'Well, then, I'll say *ta-ta*, till dinner-time;' and he went off at a good swinging pace.

'Almost looks as if they were watching me,' muttered the young officer, as he trudged on. 'Tchah! no! The old boys wouldn't do that, either of them;' and he turned into one of the thickest portions of the wood.

The major kept on rubbing his little steel trowel

till long after it was dry, and then slowly sheathed it, as if it were a sword, before going thoughtfully on hunting up various specimens of the singular plants that he made his study.

'It's very curious,' he mused, 'very. Women are unmistakably enigmas, and I suppose that things must take their course. Bless me! I must want some of his training. It's very warm.'

He stopped, took out his handkerchief, a genuine Indian bandanna, that he had brought home himself years ago, and now very soft and pleasant to the touch, but decidedly the worse for wear. He wiped his face, took off his hat, and had a good dab at his forehead, and then, after a few minutes' search round the bole of a huge beech, whose bark was ornamented with patches of lovely cream and grey lichens, he stopped short to look at a great broad buttress-like root, which spread itself in so tempting a way that it suggested a comfortable garden seat, a great favourite of the major's. Then, with a smile of satisfaction, the old man sat down, shuffled himself about a little, and finally found it so agreeable, with his back resting against the tree, that he fell into a placid state of musing on the various specimens he had collected; from them he began to think of his niece, then of Lucy Alleyne, and then of Rolph, returning to his niece by a natural sequence, and then thinking extremely deeply of nothing.

It was wonderfully quiet out there in the woods.

Now and then a bird chirped, and the harsh caw of a rook, softened by distance, was heard. Anon there came a tap on the ground, as if something had fallen from high up in the big tree, and then, after a pause, there was a rustle and swishing about of twigs and leaves, as something bounded from bough to bough, ran lightly along the bigger branches, and finally stopped, gazing with bright, dark eyes at the sleeping intruder. The latter made no sign, so after a while, the squirrel gave its beautiful, bushy tail a few twitches, uttered a low, impatient sound that resembled the chopping of wood on a block, and then scurried down the bole of the tree, picked up something, and ran off.

Soon after a rabbit came cantering among the leaves, sat up, raising it ears stiffly above its head, drooped its fore paws, and stared in turn at the sleeper, till, gaining confidence from his motionless position, it played about, ran round, gave two or three leaps from the ground, and then proceeded to nibble at various succulent herbs that grew just outside the drip from the branches of the beech.

The rabbit disappeared in turn, and after picking up a worm that had slipped out of the ground, consequent upon the rabbit having given a few scratches, in one place, a round-eyed robin flitted to a low, bare twig of the beech, and sat inspecting the major, as if he were one of the children lost in the wood, and it was necessary to calculate how many leaves it

would take to cover him before the task was com-
menced.

The delicious, scented silence of the wood continued for long enough, and then closely following
each other, with a peculiarly silent flight, half-a-
dozen grey birds came down a green arcade straight
for the great beech, where one of them, with vivid
blue edges to its wings, all lined with black, and a
fierce black pair of moustachios, set up its loose,
speckled, warm grey crest, and uttered a most de-
monically harsh cry of '*schah-tchah-tchah!*' taking
flight at once, followed by its companions, giving
vent to the same harsh scream in reply, and making
the major start from his nap, spring up, and stare
about.

'Jays!' he cried. 'Bless my soul, I must have
been asleep.'

He pulled out his watch, glanced at it, muttered
something about 'a good hour,' which really was
under the mark, and then, after a glance at his
specimens and a re-arrangement of his creel, he
started to trudge back to the Hall, but stopped and
hesitated.

'Too far that way,' he said. 'I'll try the road and
the common.'

He glanced at the tiny pocket compass attached
to his watch-chain, and started off once more in a
fresh direction, one which he knew would bring him
out on the road near Lindham. The path he soon

found was one evidently rarely used, and deliciously
soft and mossy to his feet, as, refreshed by his nap,
he went steadily on, following the windings till he
stopped short wonderingly, surprised by eye and ear,
for as he went round a sudden turn it was to find
himself within a yard or two of a girl seated on the
mossy ground, her arms clasping her knees, and her
face bent down upon them, sobbing as if her heart
would break.

' My good girl,' cried the chivalrous major eagerly.

Before he could say more, the woman's head was
raised, so that in the glance he obtained he saw that
she was young, dark and handsome, in spite of her
red and swollen eyes, dishevelled, dark hair, and
countenance generally disfigured by a passionate
burst of crying.

For a moment the girl seemed about to bound up
and run ; but she checked the impulse, clasped her
knees once more, and hid her face upon them.

' Why, I ought to know your face,' said the
major. ' Mr Rolph's keeper's daughter, if I am not
mistaken ? '

There was no reply, only a closer hiding of the
face, and a shiver.

' Can I do anything for you ? ' said the major
kindly. ' Is anything the matter ? '

' No. Go away ! ' cried the girl in low, muffled
tones.

' But you are in trouble.'

'Go away!' cried the girl fiercely ; and this she reiterated so bitterly that the major shrugged his shoulders and moved off a step or two.

'Are you sure I cannot assist you?' said the major, hesitating about leaving the girl in her trouble.

'Go away, I tell you.'

'Well then, will you tell me where to find the Lindham road?'

For answer she averted her head from him and pointed in one direction. This he followed, found the road and the open common, coming out close to a cottage to which he directed his steps in search of a cup of water.

The door was half open, and as soon as his steps approached, an old woman's sharp voice exclaimed,—

'Ah, you've come back then, you hussy! Who was that came and called you out, eh?'

'You are making a mistake,' said the major quietly. 'I came to ask if I could have a glass of water?'

'Oh yes, come in, whoever you are, if you ar'n't afraid to see an ugly old woman lying in bed. I thought it was my grandchild. Who are you?'

'I come from Brackley,' said the major, smiling down at the crotchety old thing in the bed.

'Do you? oh, then I know you. Your one of old Sir John Day's boys. Be you the one who went sojering?'

'Yes, I'm the one,' said the major, smiling.

'Ah, you've growed since then. My master pointed you out to me one day on your pony. Yes, to be sure, you was curly-headed then. There, you can take some water; it's in the brown pitcher, and yonder's a mug. It was fresh from the well two hours ago. That gal had just fetched it when some one throwed a stone at the door, and she went out to see who threw it, she said. Ah, she don't cheat me, a hussy. She knowed, and I mean to know. It was some chap, that's who it was, some chap—Caleb Kent maybe—and I'm not going to have her come pretending to do for me, and be running after gipsy chaps.'

'No, you must take care of the young folks,' said the major. 'What beautiful water!'

'Yes, my master dug that well himself, down to the stone, and it's beautiful water. Have another mug? That's right. You needn't give me anything for it without you like; but a shilling comes in very useful to get a bit o' tea. I often wish we could grow tea in one's own garden.'

'It would be handy,' said the major. 'There's half-a-crown for you, old lady. It's a shame that you should not have your bit of tea. Good-bye.'

'Good-bye to you, and thank you kindly,' cried the old woman; 'and if you see that slut of a girl just you send her on to me.'

'I will,' he said. 'Good-bye.'

'Good-bye,' shrieked the old woman; and as the major passed out of the gate, the shrill voice came after him, 'Mind you send her on if you see her.'

The words reached a second pair of ears, those of Judith, who flushed up hot and angry as she found herself once more in the presence of the major.

'You've been telling her about me,' she cried fiercely. 'It's cowardly; it's cruel.'

She stood up before him so flushed and handsome that the major felt as it were the whole of her little story.

'No,' he said quietly, 'I have not told your grand-mother about you; she has been telling me.'

With an angry, indignant look the girl swept by him and entered the cottage.

'Poor lass, she is very handsome,' said the major to himself, 'and it seems as if her bit of life romance is not going so smoothly as it should. Hah! that was a capital drop of water; it gives one life. Crying in the woods, eh—after a signal that the old lady heard. Gipsy lad, eh? Bad sign—bad sign. Ah, well,' he added, with a sigh, 'I'm getting too old a man to think of love affairs; but, somehow, I often wonder now that I did not marry.'

That thought came to him several times as he walked homeward over the boggy common, and rose again more strongly as he came in sight of The Firs and the grim, black mansion on the hillock. Fort

Science, as he had jestingly called it, looked at times bright and sunny, and then dull, repulsive and cold.

The major reached home after his very long walk rather out of spirits ; and his valet, unasked, fetched him a cup of tea.

CHAPTER X.

LUCY EXAMINES THE EXAMINER.

' I WISH you would be more open with me, Moray,' said Lucy to her brother.

He was gazing through one of his glasses intently upon some celestial object, for the night was falling fast, and first one and then another star came twinkling out in the cold grey of the north-east.

Alleyne raised his head slowly and looked at his sister's pretty enquiring face for a few moments, and then resumed his task.

' Don't understand you,' he said quietly.

' Now, Moray, you must,' cried Lucy, pettishly; ' you have only one sister, and you ought to tell her everything.'

As she spoke, in a playful, childish way, she began tying knots in her brother's long beard, and made an attempt to join a couple of threads behind his head, but without result, the crisp curly hairs being about half-an-inch too short.

Alleyne paid no heed to her playful tricks for a time, and she went on,—

137

'If I were a man—which, thank goodness, I am
not—I'd try to be learned, and wise, and clever, but
I'd be manly as well, and strong and active, and able
to follow all out-door pursuits.'

'Like Captain Rolph,' said Alleyne, with a smile,
half reproach, half satire.

'No,' cried Lucy, emphatically; 'he is all animal-
ism. He has all the strength that I like to see, and
nothing more. No, the man I should like to be,
would combine all that energy with the wisdom of
one who thinks, and uses his brains. Captain Rolph,
indeed!'

What was meant for a withering, burning look of
scorn appeared on Lucy's lips; but it was only pretty
and provocative; it would not have scorched a
child.

'No, dear, the man I should like to be would be
something very different from him. There, I don't
care what you say to the contrary, you love Glynne,
and I shall tell her so.'

'You love your brother too well ever to degrade
him in the eyes of your friend, Lucy,' said Alleyne,
drawing her to him, and stroking her hair. 'Even if
—if—'

'There, do say it out, Moray. If you did or do
love her. I do wish you wouldn't be so girlish and
weak.'

'Am I girlish and weak?' he said thoughtfully.

'Yes, and dreamy and strange, when you, who are

such a big fine-looking fellow, might be all that a woman could love.'

'All that a woman could love?' he said thoughtfully.

'Yes; instead of which you neglect yourself and go shabby and rough, and let your hair grow long. Oh, if I only could make you do what I liked. Come now, confess; you are very fond of Glynne?'

He looked at her dreamily for a while, but did not reply. It was as though his thoughts were busy upon something she had said before, and it was not until Lucy was about to speak that he checked her.

'Yes,' he said, 'you are right; I have given up everything to my studies. I have neglected myself, my mother, you, Lucy. What would you say if I were to change?'

'Oh, Moray!' she cried, catching his hands; 'and will you?—for Glynne's sake.'

'Hush!' he cried sternly; and his brows knit, as he looked down angrily in her face. 'Lucy, you wish me to be strong; if I am to be, you must never speak like that again. I have been weak, and in my weakness I have listened to your girlish prattle about your friend. Have you forgotten that she is to be— Captain Rolph's wife?'

'No,' cried Lucy impetuously, ' I have not forgotten; I never can forget it ; but if she ever is his wife, she will bitterly repent it to the end.'

Hush!' he exclaimed again, and his eyes grew

more stern, and there was a quiver of his lip. 'Let there be an end of this.'

'But do you not see that he is unworthy of her—that his tastes are low and contemptible; that he cannot appreciate her in the least, and—and besides, dear, he—he—is not honest and faithful.'

'How do you know this?' cried Alleyne sternly. Lucy flushed crimson.

'I know it by his ways—by his words,' she said, recovering herself, and speaking with spirit, 'I like Glynne; I love her, dear, and it pains me more than I can say, to see her drifting towards such a fate. Why, Moray, see how she has changed of late—see how she has taken to your studies, how she hangs upon every word you say, how—oh, Moray!'

She stopped in affright, for he clutched her arm with a violence that caused her intense pain. His brow was rugged, and an angry glare shot from his eyes, while when he spoke, it was in a low husky voice.

'Lucy,' he said, 'once for all, never use such words as these to me again. There, there, little bird, I'm not very angry; but listen to me,' and he drew her to his side in a tender caressing way. 'Is this just —is this right? You ask me to be more manly and less of the dreaming student that I have been so long, and you ask me to start upon my new career with a dishonourable act—to try and presume upon the

interest your friend has taken in my pursuit to tempt
her from her duties to the man who is to be her husband.   There, let this be forgotten ; but I will do
what you wish.'

'You will, Moray?' cried Lucy, who was now sobbing.

'Yes,' he cried, as he hid from himself the motive
power that was energising his life. 'Yes, I will now be
a man. I will show you—the world—that one can be a
great student and thinker, and at the same time a
man of that world—a gentleman of this present day.
The man who calculates the distance of one of the
glorious orbs I have made my study, rarely is as
others are in manners and discourse—educated in the
ordinary pursuits of life—without making himself ridiculous if he mounts a horse—absurd if he has to
stand in competition with his peers.   Yes, you are
right, Lucy, I have been a dreaming recluse ; now the
dreams shall be put away, and I will awaken into this
new life.'

Lucy clapped her hands, and, flinging her arms
round her brother kissed him affectionately, and then
drew her face back to gaze in his.

'Why, Moray,' she cried proudly, 'there isn't such a
man for miles as you would be, if you did as others do.'

He laughed as he kissed her, and then gently put
her away.

'There,' he said, 'go now.   I have something here
—a calculation I must finish.'

'And now you are going back to your figures again?' she cried pettishly.

'Yes, for a time,' he replied; 'but I will not forget my promise.'

'You will not?' she cried.

'I give you my word,' he said, and kissing him affectionately once again, Lucy left the observatory.

'He has forbidden me to speak,' she said to herself, with a glow of triumph in her eyes, 'but it will come about all the same. He loves Glynne with all his heart, and the love of such a man as he is cannot change. Glynne is beginning, too; and when she quite finds it out, she will never go and swear faith to that miserable Rolph. I am going to wait and let things arrange themselves, as I'm sure they will.'

The object of her thoughts was not going on with the astronomical calculation, but pacing the observatory to and fro, with his brow knit, and a feverish energy burning in his brain.

CHAPTER XI.

THE DOCTOR BRINGS ALLEYNE DOWN.

ABOUT an hour later Oldroyd called; and, as the bell jangled at the gate and Eliza went slowly down, Lucy's face turned crimson, and she ran to the window and listened, to hear the enquiry,—' Is your mistress in ?'

That was enough. The whole scene of that particular morning walk came back with a repetition of the agony of mind. She saw Rolph in his ludicrous undress, striding along the sandy road; she heard again his maundering civilities, and she saw, too, the figure of Oldroyd seated upon the miller's pony, passing them, and afterwards blocking the way.

It was he, now, seated upon the same pony; and, without waiting to hear Eliza's answer, Lucy fled to her bedroom and locked herself in, to begin sobbing and crying in the most ridiculous manner.

' No, sir,' said Eliza, with a bob; 'she've gone to town shopping, but Miss Lucy's in the drawing-room.'

Eliza smiled to herself as she said this, giving herself the credit of having managed a splendid little bit of diplomacy, for, according to her code, young gents ought to have opportunities to talk to young ladies whenever there was a chance. She was, however, terribly taken aback by the young doctor's words.

'Thank you, yes, but I don't want to see her,'—words which, had she heard them, would have made Lucy's sobs come more quickly. 'Is Mr Alleyne in?'

'Yes, sir, he's in the observatory.'

'I'll come in then,' said Oldroyd; and he dismounted, and threw the rein over the ring hook in the yard wall.

'If you please, sir,' said the maid, who did not like to lose an opportunity now that a medical man was in the house, 'I don't think I'm very well.'

'Eh, not well?' said Oldroyd, pausing in the hall, 'why you appear as rosy and bonny as a girl can look.'

'Thankye, sir,' said the girl, with a bob; 'but I'm dreadful poorly, all the same.'

'Why, what's the matter?'

For answer Eliza put her hands behind her, and seemed as if she were indulging in the school-girl trick of what is called 'making a face' at the doctor, for she closed her eyes, opened her mouth, wrinkled her brow, and put out a very long red tongue, which quivered and curled up at the point.

That'll do,' said Oldroyd, hiding a smile; and the

tongue shot back, Eliza's eyes opened, her mouth closed, and the wrinkles disappeared from her face.

'Will that do, sir?'

'Yes; your tongue's beautifully healthy, your eyes are bright, and your skin moist and cool. Why, what's the matter?'

'Please sir, I'm quite well of a night,' said Eliza, with another bob, 'but I do have such dreadful dreams.'

'Oh!' said Oldroyd, drawing in a long breath, 'I see. Did you have a bad dream last night?'

'Oh yes, sir, please. I dreamed as a poacher were going to murder me, and I couldn't run away.'

'Let me see; you had supper last night at half-past nine, did you not?'

'Yes, sir.'

'Bread and Dutch cheese?'

'Yes, sir.'

'Ah, you want a little medicine,' said Oldroyd quietly. 'I'll send you some.'

'And please, sir, how am I to take it?'

'Oh, you'll find that on the bottle, and mind this: you are not to eat any more cheese for supper, but you may have as much butter as you like, and stale bread.'

'Thank you, sir. Will you go in, sir?'

'Yes, I'll go up,' said Oldroyd, and then to himself, 'What humbugs we doctors are; but we are obliged to be. If I told the girl only to leave off eating cheese she would think she was ill-used, and as likely as not she would get a holiday on purpose to go over to the town and see another man.'

He tapped sharply on the door with the handle of his whip, and in response to the loud 'Come in,' entered, to find Alleyne standing amongst his instruments.

'Ah, Oldroyd,' he said, holding out his hand, which the other took, 'glad to see you.'

'And I'm glad to see you — looking so much better,' said Oldroyd. 'Why, man, your brain has been working in a new direction; your eyes don't look so dreamy, and the balance is getting right. Come, confess, don't you feel more energetic than you did?'

'Ten times,' said Alleyne frankly.

'Then you'll end by being a firm believer in my system—cure without drugs, eh?'

'Indeed I shall,' said Alleyne, smiling.

'And to show how consistent I am,' said Oldroyd, 'I've just promised to send your maid a bottle of medicine. But come, sir, I'm just off among the hills to see a patient. It's a lovely day; only about six miles. Come with me, and I'll leave the pony and walk.'

Alleyne shook his head.

'No,' he said, 'I should be very poor company for you, Oldroyd—yes, I will go,' he cried, recollecting himself. 'Wait a minute and I'll be back.'

'All right,' replied the doctor, who amused himself peeping among the various glasses till Alleyne came back in a closely-fitting shooting jacket, for which he had changed the long, loose dressing-gown he had worn.

'That's better,' cried Oldroyd, approvingly; 'why, Alleyne, you will be worth two of the patients I saw a few months ago if you go on like this.'

Alleyne smiled sadly, and took a soft felt hat from its peg; and as he did so, he sent his hand again to his long, wild hair, and thought of his sister's words, the colour coming into his cheeks, as he said in an assumed easy-going manner,—

'It's time I had my hair cut.'

'Well, not to put too fine a point upon it, Alleyne, it really is. I like short hair, it is so comfortable on a windy day.'

The colour stayed in Alleyne's cheeks, for, in spite of himself, he felt a little nettled that his companion should have noticed this portion of his personal appearance; but he said nothing, and they went out into the yard, where, unfastening the pony, Oldroyd threw the rein over the docile little creature's neck and then tied it to a loop in the saddle, after which the pony followed them like a dog, till they reached its stable, where it was left.

'Now,' cried Oldroyd, 'what do you say to a good tonic?'

'Do I need one?' said Alleyne, looking at him wistfully.

'Badly. I don't mean physic, man,' laughed Oldroyd, 'but a strong dose of fresh air off the hills.'

Alleyne laughed, and they started off across the boggy heath, avoiding the soft places, and, wherever the ground was firm, striding along at a good brisk pace over the elastic turf, which seemed to communicate its springiness to their limbs, while the sweet breeze sent a fresh light into their eyes.

Over the common and up the hilly lanes, where, as they went more slowly, Oldroyd told the history of his patient up at the common, the result of which was an animated discussion upon the game laws, and Oldroyd began wondering at the change that had come over his companion. He had taken in a new accession of nervous force, which lent animation to his remarks, and, as he noted all this, Oldroyd began wondering, for he frankly told himself that there must have been other influences at work to make this change.

'Isn't that Captain Rolph?' he said suddenly, as they turned into a long lane that ran through one of the pine woods on the slope of a hill.

'Rolph?' said Alleyne quietly, as he glanced in the direction of a distant horseman, coming towards them. 'Yes—no—I cannot say.'

'I should say—yes, from his military seat in the saddle,' said Oldroyd. 'Well, if it be or no, he doesn't mean to meet us. He has gone through the wood.'

For, as he spoke, the coming horseman drew rein turned his horse's head, leaped a ditch, and disappeared amongst the pines.

'What does he want up here?' said Oldroyd to himself, and then aloud, 'Been having a good "breather" round the hills,' he continued. 'Sort of thing you ought to cultivate, Alleyne. Nothing like horse exercise.'

'Horses are costly, and the money I should spend upon a horse would be valuable to me for some optical instrument,' said Alleyne, speaking cheerfully, though all the while he was slightly excited by the sight of the horseman they had supposed to be Rolph ; but this wore off in a few minutes, and they soon came in sight of the cottages, while before them a tall figure, graceful in appearance, in spite of the homely dress, had suddenly crossed a stile, hurried in the same direction, and turned in at the cottage gate.

'Mademoiselle Judith,' said Oldroyd; 'a very pretty girl with a very ugly name. Hallo! We are in trouble.'

'I don't know what's come to you. Here's your poor father so bad he can't lift hand or foot, and you always running off to Mother Wattley's or picking flowers. Flowers indeed! Better stop and mind your father.'

This in very much strident tones from the cottage whose gate they were entering ; and then a sudden

softening as Oldroyd and Alleyne darkened the
doorway, and the nurse dropped a curtsey.

'Didn't know you was so close, sir. I was only
saying a word to Judith—oh, she's gone.'

'How is Hayle to-day?' said Oldroyd, as the girl
stepped out at the back door.

'Well, sir, thank you kindly, I think he's better; he
talks stronger like, and he took a basin of hare soup
to-day, well, that he did, and it was nice and strong.'

'Hare soup, eh?' said Oldroyd, with a queer look
at Alleyne.

'Yes, sir, hare soup; he said as how he was sick o'
rabbits, and Caleb Kent kindly brought in a fine
hare for him, and—'

She stopped short, looking guiltily at the young
doctor, and two red spots came in her yellow sunken
cheeks.

'You're letting the cat—I mean the hare—out of
the bag,' said Oldroyd drily. 'One of Sir John
Day's hares?'

'Oh, sir!' faltered the woman, 'it's nothing to him;
and I'm only the nurse.'

'There, I don't want to know,' said Oldroyd. 'Can
I go up?'

'Oh yes, sir, please,' cried the woman, who was
only too glad to change the conversation after her
lapse, 'you'll find him nice and tidy.'

'Care to come and see my patient, Alleyne?' said
Oldroyd.

'Thanks, yes, I may as well,' and he followed the doctor up into the low room, where the truth of the woman's assertions were plainly to be seen. The wounded man, lying upon coarse linen that was exquisitely clean, while the partially covered boards were as white as constant scrubbing could make them.

'Well, Hayle, how are you going on? I've brought a friend of mine to see you.'

The man whose eyes and cheeks were terribly sunken, and who looked worn out with his late journey to the very gates of death, from which he was slowly struggling back, raised one big gnarled hand heavily to his forelock, and let it fall again upon the bed.

'Steady, sir, steady. Glad to see you, sir, glad to see him, sir. He's welcome like. Sit you down, sir; sit you down.'

Alleyne took the stool that was nearest and sat down watching the man curiously, as Oldroyd examined his bandages, and then asked a few questions.

'You're going on right enough,' he said at last. 'Capitally.'

'But I'm so weak, sir,' said the great helpless fellow, piteously. 'I'm feeble as a child. I can hardly just hold my hand to my head.'

'Well, what can you expect?' said Oldroyd. 'You lost nearly every drop of blood in your body, and it will take time to build you up again—to fill you up again,' he added, smiling.

'Yes sir, of course, sir; but can't you give me a bottle or two of nothing as will set me to rights? We'll pay you, you know, sir, don't you be afraid o' that.'

'Oh, I'm not afraid of that,' said Oldroyd, smiling, 'but I can give you nothing better than I am giving you. The best medicine you can have now is plenty of strong soup, the same as you had this morning.'

'Did she tell you I had soup this morning, sir?'

'Yes—hare soup,' said Oldroyd meaningly.

'Did that woman say hare soup, sir?'

'Yes, and that you were tired of rabbits. I say, Hayle, I ought to tell Sir John's keepers.'

'Eh, but you won't, sir,' said the man quietly.

'Why not?'

''Cause you're too much of a gen'leman, sir, and so would your friend be, or else you wouldn't have brought him. She needn't have let out about it, though. I'm lying helpless-like here, and they talk and do just as they like. Was my Judith downstairs, sir?'

'Yes,' said Oldroyd.

'That's a comfort,' said the man, with a sigh of content. 'Young, sir, and very pretty,' he added apologetically, to Alleyne; 'makes me a bit anxious about her, don't you see, being laid-by like. You'll come and see me again soon, doctor?'

'Yes, and I must soon have a bottle or two of port wine for you. I can't ask Sir John Day, can I?'

'No, sir, don't ask he,' said the man, with a faint smile. 'Let's play as fair as we can. If you say I'm to have some wine, we'll get it; but I'd a deal rayther have a drop of beer.'

'I daresay you would, my friend,' cried Oldroyd, smiling; 'but no beer for a long time to come. Alleyne, would you mind going down now, and sending me up the nurse?'

Alleyne rose, and, going down, sent up the woman to find himself alone with the girl of whom they had been speaking.

Student though he was, the study of woman was one that had never come beneath Alleyne's ken, and he found himself—for perhaps the first time in his life—interested, and wondering how it was that so handsome and attractive a girl could be leading so humble a cottage life as hers.

Judith, too, seemed attracted towards him, and once or twice she opened her lips and was about to speak, but a step overhead, or the movement of a chair, made her shrink away and begin busying herself in arranging chairs or the ornaments upon the chimney-piece, which she dusted and wiped.

'So you've been flower-gathering,' said Alleyne, to break a rather awkward silence.

'Yes, sir, and—' but just then Oldroyd was heard speaking at the top of the stairs, and Judith seemed to shrink within herself as he came down.

'Ah, Miss Judith, you there? Well, your father

is getting on splendidly. Take care of him. Ready, Alleyne?'

His companion rose, said good-morning to Judith, and stepped out, while Oldroyd obeyed a sign made by the girl, and stayed behind.

'Well,' he said, looking at her curiously.

'I'm so anxious about father, sir,' she said, in a low voice. 'Now that he is getting better, will there be any trouble? I mean about the keepers, and—and ' —she faltered—' the police.'

'No,' said Oldroyd, looking fixedly at the girl, till she coloured warmly beneath his stern gaze, 'everything seems to have settled down, and I don't think there is anything to fear for him. Let me speak plainly, my dear. Lookers on see most of the game.'

'I—I don't understand you, sir,' she said, colouring.

'Then try to. It seems to me that, to use a strong expression, some one has been squared. There are friends at court. Now, take my advice: as soon as father is quite well, take him into your confidence, and persuade him to go quite away. I'm sure it would be better for you both. Good-day.'

The doctor nodded and went off after Alleyne, while Judith sat down to bury her face in her hands and sob as if her heart would break.

CHAPTER XII.

VENUS MORE IN THE FIELD OF VIEW.

LUCY's life about this time was not a happy one. Mrs Alleyne was cold and distant, Moray was growing more silent day by day, taking exercise as a duty, working or walking furiously, as if eager to get the duty done, so as to be able to drown harassing thoughts in his studies; hence he saw little of, and said little to his sister. The major looked stern when he met her, and Lucy's sensitive little bosom heaved when she noticed his distant ways. Sir John, too, appeared abrupt and distant, not so friendly as of old, or else she thought so; and certainly Glynne was not so cordial, seeming to avoid her, and rarely now sending over one of her old affectionate notes imploring her to come to lunch and spend the day.

'Philip Oldroyd always looks at me as if I were a school girl,' Lucy used to cry impetuously when she was alone, 'and as if about to scold me for not wanting to learn my lessons. How dare he look at me like that, just as if there was anything between us, and he had a right!'

Then Lucy would have a long cry and take herself

to task for speaking of the doctor as *Philip* Oldroyd, and, after a good sob, feel better.

Rolph was the only one of her acquaintances who seemed to be pleasant with her, and his pleasantry she disliked, avoiding him when she went out for a walk, but generally finding him in the way, ready to place himself at her side, and walk wherever she did.

Lucy planted barbed verbal arrows in the young officer's thick hide, but the only effect of these pungent little attacks was to tickle him. He was not hurt in the slightest degree. In fact he enjoyed it under the impression that Lucy admired him immensely, and was ready to fall at his feet at any time, and declare her love.

'She doesn't know anything,' he had mused. 'Her sleepy brother noticed nothing, and as for the doctor—curse the doctor, let him mind his own business, or I'll wring his neck. I could,' he added thoughtfully, 'and I would.'

'Bah! it's only a bit of flirtation, and the little thing is so clever and sharp and piquant that she's quite a treat after a course of mushrooms with the major, and pigs and turnips with Sir John. If Alleyne should meet us—well, I met his sister, Glynne's friend, and we were chatting—about Glynne of course. And as to the doctor, well, curse the doctor, as aforesaid. I believe the beast's jealous, and I'll make him worse before I'm done.'

In Rolph's musings about Lucy he used to call her 'little pickles' and 'the sauce.' Once he got as far as 'Cayenne,' a name that pleased him immensely, making up his mind, what little he had, to call her by one of those epithets—some day—when they grew a little more warmly intimate.

On the other hand, when Lucy went out walking, it was with the stern determination to severely snub the captain, pleasant as she told herself it would be to read Philip Oldroyd a good severe lesson, letting him see that she was not neglected; and then for the moment all her promises were forgotten, till she was going home again, when the only consolation she could find for her lapse was that her intentions had been of the most stringent kind; that she could not help meeting the captain, and that she really had tried all she could to avoid him ; while there was the satisfaction of knowing that she was offering herself up as a kind of sacrifice upon the altar of duty for her brother's welfare.

'Sooner or later dear Glynne must find out what a wretch that Rolph is, and then I shall be blamed—she'll hate me; but all will be made happy for poor Moray.'

The consequence of all this was that poor Lucy about this time felt what an American would term very 'mean' and ashamed of herself; mingled with this, too, was a great deal of sentiment. She was going to be a martyr—she supposed that she would die, the fact being that Lucy was very sick—sick at heart, and there was only one doctor in the world who could put her right.

Of course the thoughts turn here to the magnates of Harley and Brook and Grosvenor Street, and of Cavendish Square, but it was none of these. The prescription that would cure Lucy's ailment was of the unwritten kind : it could only be spoken. The doctor to speak it was Philip Oldroyd, and its effect instantaneous, and this Lucy very well knew. But, like all her kind, she had a tremendous antipathy to physic, and, telling herself that she hated the doctor and all his works, she went on suffering in silence like the young lady named Viola, immortalised by one Shakespeare, and grievously sick of the same complaint.

It came like a surprise to Lucy one morning to receive a note from Glynne, written in a playful, half-chiding strain, full of reproach, and charging her with forgetting so old a friend.

'When it's all her fault!' exclaimed Lucy, as she read on, to find Glynne was coming on that afternoon. 'But Captain Rolph is sure to come with her, and that will spoil all. I declare I'll go out. No, I won't. I'll stop, and I'll be a martyr again, and stay and talk to him if it will make poor Moray happy, for I don't care what becomes of me now.'

Somehow, though, Lucy looked very cheerful that day, her eyes flashing with excitement ; and it was evident that she was making plans for putting into execution at the earliest opportunity.

As it happened, Mrs Alleyne announced that she was going over to the town on business, and directly after the early dinner a chaise hired from one of the farmers was brought round, and the dignified lady took her place beside the boy who was to drive.

'Heigho!' sighed Lucy, as she stood watching the gig with its clumsy, ill-groomed horse, and the shock-headed boy who drove, and compared the turn-out with the spic-and-span well-ordered vehicles that were in use at Brackley; and then she went down the garden thinking how nice it was to have money, or rather its products, and of how sad it was that Moray's pursuits should always be making such heavy demands upon their income, and never pay anything back.

In spite of the dreariness of the outer walls of the house, the garden at The Firs had its beauties.

It was not without its claims to be called a wilderness still, but it was a pleasant kind of wilderness now, since it had been put in order, for it sloped down as steeply as the scarped side of some fortified town, and from the zigzagged paths a splendid view could be had over the wild common in fine weather, though it was a look-out over desolation in the wintry wet.

For a great change had been wrought in this piece of ground since Moray had delved in it, and bent his back to weed and fill barrows with the accumulated growth of years. There was quite a charm about the place, and the garden seat or two, roughly made out of rustic materials, had been placed in the most tempting of positions, shaded by the old trees that had been planted generations back, but which the sandy soil had kept stunted and dense.

But the place did not charm Lucy; it only made her feel more desolate and low spirited, for turn which way she would, she knew that while the rough laborious work had been done by her brother, Oldroyd's was the brain that had suggested all the improvements, his the hand that had cut back the wild tangle of brambles, that overgrown mass of ivy, placed the chairs and seats in these selected nooks where the best views could be had, and nailed up the clematis and jasmine that the western gales had torn from their hold.

Go where she would, there was something to remind her of Oldroyd, and at last she grew, in spite of her self-command, so excited that she stopped short in dismay.

'I shall make myself ill,' she cried, half aloud; 'and if I am ill, mamma will send for Mr Oldroyd; and, oh!'

Lucy actually blushed with anger, and then turned pale with dread, as in imagination she saw herself turned into Philip Oldroyd's patient, and being ordered to put out her tongue, hold forth her hand that her pulse might be felt, and have him coming to see her once, perhaps twice, every day.

With the customary inconsistency of young ladies in her state, she exclaimed, in an angry tone, full of protestation,—

'Oh, it would be horrible!' and directly after she hurried indoors.

In due time Glynne arrived, and sent the pony carriage back, saying that she would walk home.

It was a long time since she had visited at The Firs, for of late the thought of Moray Alleyne's name and his observatory had produced a strange shrinking sensation in Glynne's breast, and it was not until she had mentally accused herself of having behaved very badly to Lucy in neglecting her so much that she had made up her mind to drive over ; but now that the girls did meet the greeting between them was very warm, and the embrace in which they indulged long and affectionate.

'Why, you look pale, Glynne, dear,' cried Lucy, forgetting her own troubles, in genuine delight at seeing her old friend as in the days of their great intimacy.

'And you, Lucy, you are quite thin,' retorted Glynne. 'You are not ill?'

'Oh, no!' cried Lucy, laughing. 'I was never better; but, really, Glynne, you don't seem quite well.'

Glynne's reply was as earnest an assurance that

she never enjoyed better health than at that present moment; and as she made this assurance she was watching Lucy narrowly, and thinking that, on the strength of the rumours she had heard from time to time, she ought to be full of resentment and dislike for her old friend, while, strange to say, she felt nothing of the kind.

'Mamma will be so sorry that she was away, Glynne,' said Lucy at last, in the regular course of conversation. 'She likes you so very much.'

'Does she?' said Glynne, dreamily.

'Oh yes; she talks about you a great deal, but Moray somehow never mentions your name.'

'Indeed!' said Glynne quietly, 'why should he?'

'Oh, I don't know,' said Lucy, watching her anxiously, and wondering whether she knew how often Captain Rolph had met her out in the lanes, and by the common side. 'He seemed to like you so very much, and to take such great interest in you when you used to meet.'

Lucy watched her friend curiously, but Glynne's countenance did not tell of the thoughts that were busy within her brain.

'Poor fellow!' continued Lucy, 'he thinks of scarcely anything but his studies.'

Lucy was very fond of Glynne, she felt all the young girlish enthusiasm of her age for the graceful statuesque maiden; while in her heart of hearts Glynne had often wished she were as bright and light-hearted and merry as Lucy. All the same though, now, excellent friends as they were, there was suspicion between them, and dread, and a curious self-consciousness of guilt that made the situation feel strange; and over and over again Glynne thought it was time to go—that she had better leave, and still she stayed.

'You never say anything to me now about your engagement, dear,' said Lucy at last, and as the words left her lips the guilty colour flushed into her cheeks, and she said to herself, 'Oh! how dare I say such a thing?'

'No,' said Glynne, quietly and calmly, opening her great eyes widely and gazing full in those of her friend, but seeing nothing of the present, only trying to read her own life in the future, what time she felt a strange sensation of wonder at her position. 'No: I never talk about it to any one,' she said at last; 'there is no need.'

'No need?' exclaimed Lucy with a gasp; and she looked quite guilty, as she bent towards Glynne ready to burst into tears, and confess that she was very very sorry for what she had done—that she utterly detested Captain Rolph, and that if she had seemed to encourage him, it was in the interest of her brother and friend.

But Glynne's calm matter-of-fact manner kept her back, and she sat and stared with her pretty little face expressing puzzledom in every line.

'No; I do not care to talk about it,' said Glynne calmly, 'there is no need to discuss that which is settled.'

'Settled, Glynne?'

'Well, inevitable,' said Glynne coldly. 'When am I to congratulate you, Lucy?' she added, with a grave smile.

'Is she bantering me?' thought Lucy; and then quickly, 'Congratulate me? there is not much likelihood of that, Glynne, dear. Poor girls without portion or position rarely find husbands.'

'Indeed!' said Glynne gravely. 'Surely a portion, as you call it, is not necessary for genuine happiness?'

'No, no, of course not, dear,' cried Lucy hastily. 'But I know what you mean, and I'll answer you. No—emphatically no: there is nobody.'

'Nobody?'

'Nobody!' cried Lucy, shaking her head vigorously 'Don't look at me like that, dear,' she continued, imploringly, for she was most earnest now in her effort to make Glynne believe, if she suspected any flirtation with Rolph, that her old friend was speaking in all sincerity and truth. 'If there were anything, dear, I should be unsettled until I had told you.'

She rose quickly, laid her hands upon Glynne's shoulders, and kissed her forehead, remaining standing by her side.

'I am glad to hear you say so, Lucy,' replied Glynne, gazing frankly in her eyes, 'for I was afraid that there was some estrangement springing up between us.'

'Yes,' cried Lucy, 'you feel as I have felt. It is because you have not spoken out candidly and freely as you used to speak to me, dear.'

Glynne's forehead contracted slightly, for she winced a little before the charge, one which recalled a bitter struggle through which she had passed, and the final conquest which she felt that she had gained.

She opened her lips to speak, but no words came, for as often as friendship for Lucy urged confession, shame acted as a bar, and stopped the eager speech that was ready for escape.

No: she felt she could not speak. A cloud had come for a time across her life; but it was now gone, and she was at rest. She could not—she dared not tell Lucy her inmost thoughts, for if she did she knew that she would be condemning herself to a hard fight with a special advocate, one who would gain an easy victory in a cause which she dreaded to own had the deepest sympathy of her heart.

Just at that moment Eliza entered hastily.

'Oh, if you please, Miss, I'm very sorry, but—'

The girl stopped short. She had made up her speech on her way to the room, but had forgotten the presence of the visitor, so she broke down, with her mouth open, feeling exceedingly shamefaced and guilty, for she knew that the simple domestic trouble about which she had come was not one that ought to be blurted forth before company.

'Will you excuse me, dear?' said Lucy, and, crossing to Eliza, she followed that young lady out of the room, to hear the history of a disaster in the cooking department; some ordinary preparation, expressly designed for that most unthankful of partakers, Moray Alleyne, being spoiled.

Hardly had Lucy left her alone, and Glynne drawn a breath of relief at having time given to compose herself, than a shadow crossed the window, there was a quick step outside, and the next moment there was a hand upon the glass door that led out towards the observatory, as Alleyne entered the room.

CHAPTER XIII.

AND RETIRES BEHIND A CLOUD.

'MISS DAY! you here?' cried Alleyne, as she rose from her seat, and then as each involuntarily shrank from the other, there was a dead silence in the room —a silence so painful that the thick heavy breathing of the man became perfectly audible, and the rustle of Glynne's dress, when she drew back, seemed to be loud and strange.

Glynne had fully intended that the next time she encountered Alleyne she would be perfectly calm, and would speak to him with the quietest and most friendly ease. That which had passed was a folly, a blindness that had been a secret in each of their hearts, for granting that which had made its way to hers, she was womanly enough of perception to feel that she had inspired Lucy's brother with a hopeless passion, one that he was too true and honourable a gentleman ever to declare.

This was Glynne's belief; and, strong in her faith in self, she had planned to act in the future so that

Alleyne should find her Lucy's cordial friend—a woman who should win his reverence so that she would be for ever sacred in his eyes.

But she had not reckoned upon being thrown with him like this; and, as he stood before her, there came a hot flush of shame to fill her cheeks, her forehead and neck with colour, but only to be succeeded by a freezing sensation of despair and dread, which sent the life-blood coursing back to her very heart, leaving her trembling as if from some sudden chill.

And Alleyne?

For weeks past he had been fighting to school his madness, as he called it—his sacrilegious madness—for he told himself that Glynne should be as sacred to him as if she were already Rolph's honoured wife, while now, coming suddenly upon her as he had, and seeing the agitation which his presence caused, every good resolution was swept away. He did not see Rolph's promised wife before him; he did not see the woman whom he had, in his inmost heart, vowed a hundred times to look upon as the idol of some dream of love, an unsubstantial fancy, whom he could never see ; but she who stood there was Glynne Day, the woman who had just taught him what it was to love. For all these years he had been the slave of science. His every thought had been given to the work of his most powerful mistress, and then the slave had revolted. Again and again he had told himself that he had resumed his allegiance, that science was his queen once more, and that he should never again stray from her paths.   That he had had his lesson, as men before him; but that he had fought bravely, manfully, and conquered; and now, as soon as he stood in presence of Glynne, his shallow defences were all swept away—he was at her mercy.

As they stood gazing at each other, Alleyne made another effort.

'I will be strong—a man who can master self.   I will not give way,' he said to himself; and even as he hugged these thoughts it was as if some mocking voice were at his elbow, whispering to him these questions,—

'Was it right that this sweet, pure-minded woman, whose thoughts were every day growing broader and higher, and who had taught him what it really was to love, should become the wife of that thoughtless, brainless creature, whose highest aim was to win the applause of a senseless mob to the neglect of everything that was great and good?

'She loves you—she who was so calm and fancy free, has she not seemed to open—unfold that pure chalice of her heart before you, to fill it to the brim with thoughts of you?   Has she not eagerly sought to follow, however distantly, in your steps; read the books you advised; thirsted for the knowledge that dropped from your lips; thrown aside the trivialities of life to take to the solid sciences you love? And why—why?—because she loves you.'

Every promise self-made, every energetic determination to be stern in his watch over self was forgotten in these moments; and it was only by a strenuous effort that he mastered himself enough to keep back for the time the flow of words that were thronging to his lips.

As it was, he walked straight to her, and caught her hand in his—a cold, trembling hand, which Glynne felt that she could not draw back. The stern commanding look in his eyes completely mastered her, and for the moment she felt that she was his very slave.

' I must speak with you,' he said, in a low, hoarse voice. ' I cannot talk here; come out beneath the sky, where the air is free and clear. Glynne, I must speak with you now.'

She made no reply, but yielded the hand he had caught in his and pressed in his emotion, till it gave her intense pain, and walked by his side as if fascinated. She was very pale now, and her temples throbbed, but no word came to her lips. She could not speak.

Alleyne walked swiftly from the room, threw open the door, and led Glynne past the window, and down one of the sloping paths, towards where a seat had been placed during the past few months, never with the intention of its being occupied by Glynne. While

he spoke, and as they were on their way, Lucy came
back into the room.

' Pray forgive me, Glynne. I— Oh!'

Lucy stopped short, with an ejaculation full of surprise and pleasure. ' It *is* coming right!' she exclaimed
—'it is coming right! Oh, I must not listen to them.
How absurd. I could not hear them if I tried. I
ought not to watch them either. But I can't help it.
It can't be very wrong. He's my own dear brother,
and I'm sure I love Glynne like a sister, and I'm sure
I pray that good may come of all this, for it would be
madness for her to think of keeping to her engagement
with that dreadful—'

Lucy stopped short, with her eyes dilated and
fixed. She had heard a sound, and turned sharply
to feel as if turned to stone; but long ere this Glynne
had been led by Alleyne to the seat, and silence had
fallen between them.

The same strange sensation of fascination was
upon Glynne. She was terror-stricken, and yet
happy; she was ready to turn and flee the moment
the influence ceased to hold her there, but meanwhile
she felt as if in a dream, and allowed her companion
to place her in the seat beneath the clustering ivy,
which was one mass of darkening berries, while he
stood before her with his hands clasped, his forehead
wrinkled, evidently the prey to some fierce emotion.

' He loves me,' whispered Glynne's heart, and there
was a sweet sensation of joy to thrill her nerves, but

only to be broken down the next moment at the call of duty ; and she sat motionless, listening as he said, roughly and hoarsely,—

'I never thought to have spoken these word to you, Glynne. I believed that I was master of myself. But they will come—I must tell you. I should not—I feel I should not, but I must—I must. Glynne—forgive me—have pity on me—I love you more than I can say.'

The spell was broken as he caught her hands in his. The sense of being fascinated had passed away, leaving Glynne Day in the full possession of her faculties, and the thought of the duty she owed another, as she started to her feet, saying words that came to her lips, not from her heart, but she knew not how they were inspired, as she spoke with all the angry dignity of an outraged woman.

'How dare you ?' she exclaimed, in a tone that made him shrink from her. 'How dare you speak to me, your sister's friend, like this? It is an insult, Mr Alleyne, and that you know.'

'How dare I ?' he cried, recovering himself. 'An insult? No, no! you do not mean this. Glynne, for pity's sake, do not speak to me such words as these.'

'Mr Alleyne, I can but repeat them,' she said excitedly, 'it is an insult, or you must be mad.'

'I thank you,' he said, changing his tone of voice, and speaking calmly, evidently by a tremendous effort over himself. 'Yes, I must be mad—you here?'

'Yes, I am here,' cried Rolph fiercely, for he had come up behind them unobserved with Lucy, who had vainly tried to stop him, following, looking white, and trembling visibly. 'What is the meaning of this? Glynne, why are you here? What has this man been saying?'

There was no reply. Alleyne standing stern and frowning, and Glynne looking wildly from one to the other unable to speak.

'I heard you say something about an insult,' cried Rolph hotly; has the blackguard dared—'

'Take me back home, Robert,' said Glynne, in a strangely altered voice.

'Then tell me first,' cried Rolph. 'How dare he speak to you, what does he mean?'

He took hold of Glynne's arm, and shook it impatiently as he spoke, but she made no reply, only looked wistfully from Rolph to Alleyne and back.

'Take me home,' she said again.

'Yes, yes, I will; but if this scoundrel has—'

'How dare you call my brother a scoundrel?' cried Lucy, firing up. 'You of all persons in the world.'

Rolph turned to her sharply, and she pointed down the path, towards the gate.

'Go!' she said; 'go directly, or I shall be tempted to tell Glynne all that I could tell her. Leave our place at once.'

Rolph glared at her for a moment, but turned from her directly, as too insignificant for his notice, and once more he exclaimed,—

'I insist on knowing what this man has said to you, Glynne—'

He did not finish his sentence, but, in the brutality of his health and strength, he looked with such lofty contempt upon the man whom he was calling in his heart 'grub,' 'bookworm,' that as Alleyne stood there bent and silent, gazing before him, straining every nerve to maintain his composure before Glynne, the struggle seemed too hard.

How mean and contemptible he must look before her, he thought—how degraded ; and as he stood there silent and determined not to resent Rolph's greatest indignity, his teeth were pressed firmly together, and his veins gathered and knotted themselves in his brow.

There was something exceedingly animal in Rolph's aspect and manner at this time, so much that it was impossible to help comparing him to an angry combative dog. He snuffed and growled audibly; he showed his teeth ; and his eyes literally glared as he appeared ready to dash at his enemy, and engage in a fierce struggle in defence of what he looked upon as his just rights.

Had Alleyne made any sign of resistance, Rolph would have called upon his brute force, and struck him ; but the idea of resenting Rolph's violence of

word and look did not occur to Alleyne. He had
sinned, he felt, socially against Glynne; he had
allowed his passion to master him, and he told himself he was receiving but his due.

The painful scene was at last brought to an end,
when once more Rolph turned to Glynne, saying
angrily,—

'Why don't you speak? Why don't you tell me
what is wrong?'

He shook her arm violently, and as he spoke
Alleyne felt a thrill of passionate anger run through
him that this man should dare to act thus, and to
address the gentle, graceful woman before him in
such a tone. It was maddening, and a prophetic
instinct made him imagine the treatment Glynne
would receive when she had been this man's wife
for years.

At last Glynne found words, and said hastily,—

'Mr Alleyne made a private communication to me.
He said words that he must now regret. That is all.
It was a mistake. Let us leave here. Take me to
my father—at once.'

Rolph took Glynne's hand, and drew it beneath his
arm, glaring at Alleyne the while like some angry
dog; but though Lucy stood there, fierce and excited,
and longing to dash into the fray as she looked from
Rolph to Glynne and back, her brother did not even
raise his eyes. A strange thrill of rage, resentment
and despair ran through him, but he could not trust

himself to meet Rolph's eye. He stood with his brow knit, motionless, as if stunned by the incidents of the past few minutes, and no words left his lips till he was alone with Lucy, who threw herself sobbing in his arms.

END OF VOL. II.

COLSTON AND COMPANY, PRINTERS, EDINBURGH.

A LIST OF NEW BOOKS AND ANNOUNCEMENTS OF METHUEN AND COMPANY PUBLISHERS : LONDON 36 ESSEX STREET W.C.

CONTENTS

OCTOBER 1894

MESSRS. METHUEN'S
ANNOUNCEMENTS

❖

Poetry

Rudyard Kipling. BALLADS. By RUDYARD KIPLING.
Crown 8vo. Buckram. 6s. [*May* 1895.
The announcement of a new volume of poetry from Mr. Kipling will excite wide
interest. The exceptional success of 'Barrack-Room Ballads,' with which this
volume will be uniform, justifies the hope that the new book too will obtain a
wide popularity.

Henley. ENGLISH LYRICS. Selected and Edited by
W. E. HENLEY. *Crown 8vo. Buckram. 6s.*
Also 30 copies on hand-made paper *Demy 8vo.* £1, 1s.
Also 15 copies on Japanese paper. *Demy 8vo.* £2, 2s.
Few announcements will be more welcome to lovers of English verse than the one
that Mr. Henley is bringing together into one book the finest lyrics in our
language. Robust and original the book will certainly be, and it will be produced with the same care that made 'Lyra Heroica' delightful to the hand and
eye.

"Q" THE GOLDEN POMP : A Procession of English Lyrics
from Surrey to Shirley, arranged by A. T. QUILLER COUCH. *Crown
8vo. Buckram. 6s.*
Also 30 copies on hand-made paper. *Demy 8vo.* £1, 1s.
Also 15 copies on Japanese paper. *Demy 8vo.* £2, 2s.
Mr. Quiller Couch's taste and sympathy mark him out as a born anthologist, and
out of the wealth of Elizabethan poetry he has made a book of great attraction.

Beeching. LYRA SACRA : An Anthology of Sacred Verse.
Edited by H. C. BEECHING, M.A. *Crown 8vo. Buckram. 6s.*
Also 25 copies on hand-made paper. 21s.
This book will appeal to a wide public. Few languages are richer in serious verse
than the English, and the Editor has had some difficulty in confining his material
within his limits.

Yeats. A BOOK OF IRISH VERSE. Edited by W. B.
YEATS. *Crown 8vo. 3s. 6d.*

Illustrated Books

Baring Gould. A BOOK OF FAIRY TALES retold by S. BARING GOULD. With numerous illustrations and initial letters by ARTHUR J. GASKIN. *Crown 8vo. 6s.*

Also 50 copies on hand-made paper. *Demy 8vo. £1, 1s.*

Also 15 copies on Japanese paper. *Demy 8vo. £2, 2s.*

Few living writers have been more loving students of fairy and folk lore than Mr. Baring Gould, who in this book returns to the field in which he won his spurs. This volume consists of the old stories which have been dear to generations of children, and they are fully illustrated by Mr. Gaskin, whose exquisite designs for Andersen's Tales won him last year an enviable reputation.

Baring Gould. A BOOK OF NURSERY SONGS AND RHYMES. Edited by S. BARING GOULD, and illustrated by the Students of the Birmingham Art School. *Crown 8vo. 6s.*

Also 50 copies on Japanese paper. *4to. 30s.*

A collection of old nursery songs and rhymes, including a number which are little known. The book contains some charming illustrations by the Birmingham students under the superintendence of Mr. Gaskin, and Mr. Baring Gould has added numerous notes.

Beeching. A BOOK OF CHRISTMAS VERSE. Edited by H. C. BEECHING, M.A., and Illustrated by WALTER CRANE. *Crown 8vo. 6s.*

Also 50 copies on hand-made paper. *Demy 8vo. £1, 1s.*

Also 15 copies on Japanese paper. *Demy 8vo. £2, 2s.*

A collection of the best verse inspired by the birth of Christ from the Middle Ages to the present day. Mr. Walter Crane has designed some beautiful illustrations. A distinction of the book is the large number of poems it contains by modern authors, a few of which are here printed for the first time.

Jane Barlow. THE BATTLE OF THE FROGS AND MICE, translated by JANE BARLOW, Author of 'Irish Idylls,' and pictured by F. D. BEDFORD. *Small 4to. 6s. net.*

Also 50 copies on Japanese paper. *4to. 30s. net.*

This is a new version of a famous old fable. Miss Barlow, whose brilliant volume of 'Irish Idylls' has gained her a wide reputation, has told the story in spirited flowing verse, and Mr. Bedford's numerous illustrations and ornaments are as spirited as the verse they picture. The book will be one of the most beautiful and original books possible.

Devotional Books

With full-page Illustrations.

THE IMITATION OF CHRIST. By THOMAS À KEMPIS. With an Introduction by ARCHDEACON FARRAR. Illustrated by C. M. GERE. *Fcap. 8vo.* 3*s.* 6*d.*

Also 25 copies on hand-made paper. 15*s.*

THE CHRISTIAN YEAR. By JOHN KEBLE. With an Introduction and Notes by W. LOCK, M.A., Sub-Warden of Keble College, Author of 'The Life of John Keble.' Illustrated by R. ANNING BELL. *Fcap. 8vo.* 5*s.*

Also 25 copies on hand-made paper. 15*s.*

These two volumes will be charming editions of two famous books, finely illustrated and printed in black and red. The scholarly introductions will give them an added value, and they will be beautiful to the eye, and of convenient size.

General Literature

Gibbon. THE DECLINE AND FALL OF THE ROMAN EMPIRE. By EDWARD GIBBON. A New Edition, edited with Notes and Appendices and Maps by J. B. BURY, M.A., Fellow of Trinity College, Dublin. *In seven volumes. Crown 8vo.*

The time seems to have arrived for a new edition of Gibbon's great work—furnished with such notes and appendices as may bring it up to the standard of recent historical research. Edited by a scholar who has made this period his special study, and issued in a convenient form and at a moderate price, this edition should fill an obvious void.

Flinders Petrie. A HISTORY OF EGYPT, FROM THE EARLIEST TIMES TO THE HYKSOS. By W. M. FLINDERS PETRIE, D.C.L., Professor of Egyptology at University College. *Fully Illustrated. Crown 8vo.* 6*s.*

This volume is the first of an illustrated History of Egypt in six volumes, intended both for students and for general reading and reference, and will present a complete record of what is now known, both of dated monuments and of events, from the prehistoric age down to modern times. For the earlier periods every trace of the various kings will be noticed, and all historical questions will be fully discussed. The volumes will cover the following periods ;—

I. Prehistoric to Hyksos times. By Prof. Flinders Petrie. II. xviiith to xxth Dynasties. III. xxist to xxxth Dynasties. IV. The Ptolemaic Rule. V. The Roman Rule. VI. The Muhammedan Rule.

The volumes will be issued separately. The first will be ready in the autumn, the Muhammedan volume early next year, and others at intervals of half a year.

Flinders Petrie. EGYPTIAN DECORATIVE ART. By W. M. FLINDERS PETRIE, D.C.L. With 120 Illustrations. *Crown 8vo. 3s. 6d.*
A book which deals with a subject which has never yet been seriously treated.

Flinders Petrie. EGYPTIAN TALES. Edited by W. M. FLINDERS PETRIE. Illustrated by TRISTRAM ELLIS. *Crown 8vo. 3s. 6d.*
A selection of the ancient tales of Egypt, edited from original sources, and of great importance as illustrating the life and society of ancient Egypt.

Southey. ENGLISH SEAMEN (Howard, Clifford, Hawkins, Drake, Cavendish). By ROBERT SOUTHEY. Edited, with an Introduction, by DAVID HANNAY. *Crown 8vo. 6s.*
This is a reprint of some excellent biographies of Elizabethan seamen, written by Southey and never republished. They are practically unknown, and they deserve, and will probably obtain, a wide popularity.

Waldstein. JOHN RUSKIN : a Study. By CHARLES WALDSTEIN, M.A., Fellow of King's College, Cambridge. With a Photogravure Portrait after Professor HERKOMER. *Post 8vo. 5s.*
Also 25 copies on Japanese paper. *Demy 8vo. 21s.*
This is a frank and fair appreciation of Mr. Ruskin's work and influence—literary and social—by an able critic, who has enough admiration to make him sympathetic, and enough discernment to make him impartial.

Henley and Whibley. A BOOK OF ENGLISH PROSE. Collected by W. E. HENLEY and CHARLES WHIBLEY. *Cr. 8vo. 6s.*
Also 40 copies on Dutch paper. *21s. net.*
Also 15 copies on Japanese paper. *42s. net.*
A companion book to Mr. Henley's well-known 'Lyra Heroica.' It is believed that no such collection of splendid prose has ever been brought within the compass of one volume. Each piece, whether containing a character-sketch or incident, is complete in itself. The book will be finely printed and bound.

Robbins. THE EARLY LIFE OF WILLIAM EWART GLADSTONE. By A. F. ROBBINS. *With Portraits. Crown 8vo. 6s.*
A full account of the early part of Mr. Gladstone's extraordinary career, based on much research, and containing a good deal of new matter, especially with regard to his school and college days.

Baring Gould. THE DESERTS OF SOUTH CENTRAL FRANCE. By S. BARING GOULD. With numerous Illustrations by F. D. BEDFORD, S. HUTTON, etc. *2 vols. Demy 8vo. 32s.*
This book is the first serious attempt to describe the great barren tableland that extends to the south of Limousin in the Department of Aveyron, Lot, etc., a country of dolomite cliffs, and cañons, and subterranean rivers. The region is full of prehistoric and historic interest, relics of cave-dwellers, of mediæval robbers, and of the English domination and the Hundred Years' War. The book is lavishly illustrated.

Baring Gould. A GARLAND OF COUNTRY SONG: English Folk Songs with their traditional melodies. Collected and arranged by S. BARING GOULD and H. FLEETWOOD SHEPPARD. *Royal 8vo.* 6s.

In collecting West of England airs for 'Songs of the West,' the editors came across a number of songs and airs of considerable merit, which were known throughout England and could not justly be regarded as belonging to Devon and Cornwall. Some fifty of these are now given to the world.

Oliphant. THE FRENCH RIVIERA. By Mrs. OLIPHANT and F. R. OLIPHANT. With Illustrations and Maps. *Crown 8vo.* 6s.

A volume dealing with the French Riviera from Toulon to Mentone. Without falling within the guide-book category, the book will supply some useful practical information, while occupying itself chiefly with descriptive and historical matter. A special feature will be the attention directed to those portions of the Riviera, which, though full of interest and easily accessible from many well-frequented spots, are generally left unvisited by English travellers, such as the Maures Mountains and the St. Tropez district, the country lying between Cannes, Grasse and the Var, and the magnificent valleys behind Nice. There will be several original illustrations.

George. BATTLES OF ENGLISH HISTORY. By H. B. GEORGE, M.A., Fellow of New College, Oxford. *With numerous Plans. Crown 8vo.* 6s.

This book, by a well-known authority on military history, will be an important contribution to the literature of the subject. All the great battles of English history are fully described, connecting chapters carefully treat of the changes wrought by new discoveries and developments, and the healthy spirit of patriotism is nowhere absent from the pages.

Shedlock. THE PIANOFORTE SONATA: Its Origin and Development. By J. S. SHEDLOCK. *Crown 8vo.* 5s.

This is a practical and not unduly technical account of the Sonata treated historically. It contains several novel features, and an account of various works little known to the English public.

Jenks. ENGLISH LOCAL GOVERNMENT. By E JENKS, M.A., Professor of Law at University College, Liverpool. *Crown 8vo.* 2s. 6d.

A short account of Local Government, historical and explanatory, which will appear very opportunely.

Dixon. A PRIMER OF TENNYSON. By W. M. DIXON, M.A., Professor of English Literature at Mason College. *Fcap. 8vo.* 1s. 6d.

This book consists of (1) a succinct but complete biography of Lord Tennyson; (2) an account of the volumes published by him in chronological order, dealing with the more important poems separately ; (3) a concise criticism of Tennyson in his various aspects as lyrist, dramatist, and representative poet of his day; (4) a bibliography. Such a complete book on such a subject, and at such a moderate price, should find a host of readers.

Oscar Browning. THE AGE OF THE CONDOTTIERI : A Short History of Italy from 1409 to 1530. By OSCAR BROWNING, M.A., Fellow of King's College, Cambridge. *Crown 8vo.* 5s.

This book is a continuation of Mr. Browning's 'Guelphs and Ghibellines,' and the two works form a complete account of Italian history from 1250 to 1530.

Layard. RELIGION IN BOYHOOD. Notes on the Religious Training of Boys. With a Preface by J. R. ILLINGWORTH. By E. B. LAYARD, M.A. 18mo. 1s.

Chalmers Mitchell. OUTLINES OF BIOLOGY. By P. CHALMERS MITCHELL, M.A., F.Z.S. *Fully Illustrated. Crown 8vo.* 6s.

A text-book designed to cover the new Schedule issued by the Royal College of Physicians and Surgeons.

Malden. ENGLISH RECORDS. A Companion to the History of England. By H. E. MALDEN, M.A. *Crown 8vo.* 3s. 6d.

A book which aims at concentrating information upon dates, genealogy, officials, constitutional documents, etc., which is usually found scattered in different volumes.

Hutton. THE VACCINATION QUESTION. A Letter to the Right Hon. H. H. ASQUITH, M.P. By A. W. HUTTON, M.A. *Crown 8vo.*

Leaders of Religion

NEW VOLUMES

Crown 8vo. 3s. 6d.

LANCELOT ANDREWES, Bishop of Winchester. By R. L. OTTLEY, Principal of Pusey House, Oxford, and Fellow of Magdalen. *With Portrait.*

ST. AUGUSTINE of Canterbury. By E. L. CUTTS, D.D. *With a Portrait.*

THOMAS CHALMERS. By Mrs. OLIPHANT. *With a Portrait. Second Edition.*

JOHN KEBLE. By WALTER LOCK, Sub-Warden of Keble College. *With a Portrait. Seventh Edition.*

English Classics

Edited by W. E. HENLEY.

Messrs. Methuen propose to publish, under this title, a series of the masterpieces of the English tongue.

The ordinary 'cheap edition' appears to have served its purpose: the public has found out the artist-printer, and is now ready for something better fashioned. This, then, is the moment for the issue of such a series as, while well within the reach of the average buyer, shall be at once an ornament to the shelf of him that owns, and a delight to the eye of him that reads.

The series, of which Mr. William Ernest Henley is the general editor, will confine itself to no single period or department of literature. Poetry, fiction, drama, biography, autobiography, letters, essays—in all these fields is the material of many goodly volumes.

The books, which are designed and printed by Messrs. Constable, will be issued in two editions—

(1) A small edition, on the finest Japanese vellum, limited in most cases to 75 copies, demy 8vo, 21s. a volume nett;

(2) The popular edition on laid paper, crown 8vo, buckram, 3s. 6d. a volume.

The first six numbers are :—

THE LIFE AND OPINIONS OF TRISTRAM SHANDY. By LAWRENCE STERNE. With an Introduction by CHARLES WHIBLEY, and a Portrait. 2 vols.

THE WORKS OF WILLIAM CONGREVE. With an Introduction by G. S. STREET, and a Portrait. 2 vols.

THE LIVES OF DONNE, WOTTON, HOOKER, HERBERT, AND SANDERSON. By IZAAK WALTON. With an Introduction by VERNON BLACKBURN, and a Portrait.

THE ADVENTURES OF HADJI BABA OF ISPAHAN. By JAMES MORIER. With an Introduction by E. S. BROWNE, M.A.

THE POEMS OF ROBERT BURNS. With an Introduction by W. E. HENLEY, and a Portrait. 2 vols.

THE LIVES OF THE ENGLISH POETS. By SAMUEL JOHNSON, LL.D. With an Introduction by JOHN HEPBURN MILLAR, and a Portrait. 3 vols.

Classical Translations

NEW VOLUMES

Crown 8vo. Finely printed and bound in blue buckram.

LUCIAN—Six Dialogues (Nigrinus, Icaro-Menippus, The Cock, The Ship, The Parasite, The Lover of Falsehood). Translated by S. T. IRWIN, M.A., Assistant Master at Clifton; late Scholar of Exeter College, Oxford. 3s. 6d.

SOPHOCLES—Electra and Ajax. Translated by E. D. A. MORSHEAD, M.A., late Scholar of New College, Oxford; Assistant Master at Winchester. 2s. 6d.

TACITUS—Agricola and Germania. Translated by R. B. TOWNSHEND, late Scholar of Trinity College, Cambridge. 2s. 6d.

CICERO—Select Orations (Pro Milone, Pro Murena, Philippic II., In Catilinam). Translated by H. E. D. BLAKISTON, M.A., Fellow and Tutor of Trinity College, Oxford. 5s.

University Extension Series

NEW VOLUMES. Crown 8vo. 2s. 6d.

THE EARTH. An Introduction to Physiography. By EVAN SMALL, M.A. *Illustrated.*

INSECT LIFE. By F. W. THEOBALD, M.A. *Illustrated.*

Social Questions of To-day

NEW VOLUME. Crown 8vo. 2s. 6d.

WOMEN'S WORK. By LADY DILKE, MISS BULLEY, and MISS WHITLEY.

Cheaper Editions

Baring Gould. THE TRAGEDY OF THE CAESARS: The Emperors of the Julian and Claudian Lines. With numerous Illustrations from Busts, Gems, Cameos, etc. By S. BARING GOULD, Author of 'Mehalah,' etc. *Third Edition. Royal 8vo.* 15s.

'A most splendid and fascinating book on a subject of undying interest. The great feature of the book is the use the author has made of the existing portraits of the Caesars, and the admirable critical subtlety he has exhibited in dealing with this line of research. It is brilliantly written, and the illustrations are supplied on a scale of profuse magnificence.'—*Daily Chronicle.*

Clark Russell. THE LIFE OF ADMIRAL LORD COLLINGWOOD. By W. CLARK RUSSELL, Author of 'The Wreck of the Grosvenor.' With Illustrations by F. BRANGWYN. *Second Edition. 8vo.* 6s.

'A most excellent and wholesome book, which we should like to see in the hands of every boy in the country.'—*St. James's Gazette.*

A 2

Fiction

Baring Gould. KITTY ALONE. By S. BARING GOULD, Author of 'Mehalah,' 'Cheap Jack Zita,' etc. 3 *vols.* *Crown 8vo.*
A romance of Devon life.

Norris. MATTHEW AUSTIN. By W. E. NORRIS, Author of 'Mdle. de Mersai,' etc. 3 *vols.* *Crown 8vo.*
A story of English social life by the well-known author of 'The Rogue.'

Parker. THE TRAIL OF THE SWORD. By GILBERT PARKER, Author of 'Pierre and his People,' etc. 2 *vols.* *Crown 8vo.*
A historical romance dealing with a stirring period in the history of Canada.

Anthony Hope. THE GOD IN THE CAR. By ANTHONY HOPE, Author of 'A Change of Air,' etc. 2 *vols.* *Crown 8vo.*
A story of modern society by the clever author of 'The Prisoner of Zenda.'

Mrs. Watson. THIS MAN'S DOMINION. By the Author of 'A High Little World.' 2 *vols.* *Crown 8vo.*
A story of the conflict between love and religious scruple.

Conan Doyle. ROUND THE RED LAMP. By A. CONAN DOYLE, Author of 'The White Company,' 'The Adventures of Sherlock Holmes,' etc. *Crown 8vo.* 6*s.*
This volume, by the well-known author of 'The Refugees,' contains the experiences of a general practitioner, round whose 'Red Lamp' cluster many dramas—some sordid, some terrible. The author makes an attempt to draw a few phases of life from the point of view of the man who lives and works behind the lamp.

Barr. IN THE MIDST OF ALARMS. By ROBERT BARR, Author of 'From Whose Bourne,' etc. *Crown 8vo.* 6*s.*
A story of journalism and Fenians, told with much vigour and humour.

Benson. SUBJECT TO VANITY. By MARGARET BENSON. With numerous Illustrations. *Crown 8vo.* 3*s.* 6*d.*
A volume of humorous and sympathetic sketches of animal life and home pets.

X. L. AUT DIABOLUS AUT NIHIL, and Other Stories. By X. L. *Crown 8vo.* 3*s.* 6*d.*
A collection of stories of much weird power. The title story appeared some years ago in 'Blackwood's Magazine,' and excited considerable attention. The 'Spectator' spoke of it as 'distinctly original, and in the highest degree imaginative. The conception, if self-generated, is almost as lofty as Milton's.'

Morrison. TALES OF MEAN STREETS. By ARTHUR MORRISON. *Crown 8vo.* 6*s.*
A volume of sketches of East End life, some of which have appeared in the 'National Observer,' and have been much praised for their truth and strength and pathos.

O'Grady. THE COMING OF CURCULAIN. By STANDISH O'GRADY, Author of 'Finn and his Companions,' etc. Illustrated by MURRAY SMITH. *Crown 8vo.* 3*s.* 6*d.*
The story of the boyhood of one of the legendary heroes of Ireland.

New Editions

E. F. Benson. THE RUBICON. By E. F. BENSON, Author of ' Dodo.' *Fourth Edition. Crown 8vo. 6s.*

Mr. Benson's second novel has been, in its two volume form, almost as great a success as his first. The ' Birmingham Post' says it is '*well written, stimulating, unconventional, and, in a word, characteristic*': the ' National Observer' congratulates Mr. Benson upon '*an exceptional achievement,*' and calls the book '*a notable advance on his previous work.*'

Stanley Weyman. UNDER THE RED ROBE. By STANLEY WEYMAN, Author of ' A Gentleman of France.' With Twelve Illustrations by R. Caton Woodville. *Fourth Edition. Crown 8vo. 6s.*

A cheaper edition of a book which won instant popularity. No unfavourable review occurred, and most critics spoke in terms of enthusiastic admiration. The ' Westminster Gazette' called it '*a book of which we have read every word for the sheer pleasure of reading, and which we put down with a pang that we cannot forget it all and start again.*' The ' Daily Chronicle' said that *every one who reads books at all must read this thrilling romance, from the first page of which to the last the breathless reader is haled along.*' It also called the book '*an inspiration of manliness and courage.*' The ' Globe' called it '*a delightful tale of chivalry and adventure, vivid and dramatic, with a wholesome modesty and reverence for the highest.*'

Baring Gould. THE QUEEN OF LOVE. By S. BARING GOULD, Author of ' Cheap Jack Zita,' etc. *Second Edition. Crown 8vo, 6s.*

The scenery is admirable and the dramatic incidents most striking.'—*Glasgow Herald.*
' Strong, interesting, and clever.'—*Westminster Gazette.*
' You cannot put it down till you have finished it.'—*Punch.*
Can be heartily recommended to all who care for cleanly, energetic, and interesting fiction.'—*Sussex Daily News.*

Mrs. Oliphant. THE PRODIGALS. By Mrs. OLIPHANT. *Second Edition. Crown 8vo. 3s. 6d.*

Richard Pryce. WINIFRED MOUNT. By RICHARD PRYCE. *Second Edition. Crown 8vo. 3s. 6d.*

The ' Sussex Daily News' called this book '*a delightful story,*' and said that the writing was '*uniformly bright and graceful.*' The ' Daily Telegraph' said that the author was a '*deft and elegant story-teller,*' and that the book was '*an extremely clever story, utterly untainted by pessimism or vulgarity.*'

Constance Smith. A CUMBERER OF THE GROUND. By CONSTANCE SMITH, Author of ' The Repentance of Paul Wentworth,' etc. *New Edition. Crown 8vo. 3s. 6d.*

School Books

A VOCABULARY OF LATIN IDIOMS AND PHRASES.
By A. M. M. STEDMAN, M.A. 18*mo.* 1*s.*

STEPS TO GREEK. By A. M. M. STEDMAN, M.A. 18*mo.*
1*s.* 6*d.*

A SHORTER GREEK PRIMER OF ACCIDENCE AND
SYNTAX. By A. M. M. STEDMAN, M.A. *Crown 8vo.* 1*s.* 6*d.*

SELECTIONS FROM THE ODYSSEY. With Introduction
and Notes. By E. D. STONE, M.A., late Assistant Master at Eton.
Fcap. 8vo. 2*s.*

THE ELEMENTS OF ELECTRICITY AND MAGNETISM.
With numerous Illustrations. By R. G. STEEL, M.A., Head Master
of the Technical Schools, Northampton. *Crown 8vo.* 4*s.* 6*d.*

THE ENGLISH CITIZEN : HIS RIGHTS AND DUTIES. By
H. E. MALDEN, M.A. *Crown 8vo.* 1*s.* 6*d.*
A simple account of the privileges and duties of the English citizen.

INDEX POETARUM LATINORUM. By E. F. BENECKE,
M.A. *Crown 8vo.* 4*s.* 6*d.*
An aid to Latin Verse Composition.

Commercial Series

A PRIMER OF BUSINESS. By S. JACKSON, M.A. *Crown
8vo.* 1*s.* 6*d.*

COMMERCIAL ARITHMETIC. By F. G. TAYLOR. *Crown
8vo.* 1*s.* 6*d.*

𝔑ew and 𝔑ecent 𝔅ooks

Poetry

Rudyard Kipling. BARRACK-ROOM BALLADS; And Other Verses. By RUDYARD KIPLING. *Seventh Edition. Crown 8vo. 6s.*

A Special Presentation Edition, bound in white buckram, with extra gilt ornament. *7s. 6d.*

'Mr. Kipling's verse is strong, vivid, full of character. . . . Unmistakable genius rings in every line.'—*Times.*

'The disreputable lingo of Cockayne is henceforth justified before the world; for a man of genius has taken it in hand, and has shown, beyond all cavilling, that in its way it also is a medium for literature. You are grateful, and you say to yourself, half in envy and half in admiration: " Here is a *book*; here, or one is a Dutchman, is one of the books of the year."'—*National Observer.*

' "Barrack-Room Ballads" contains some of the best work that Mr. Kipling has ever done, which is saying a good deal. " Fuzzy-Wuzzy," "Gunga Din," and "Tommy," are, in our opinion, altogether superior to anything of the kind that English literature has hitherto produced.'—*Athenæum.*

'These ballads are as wonderful in their descriptive power as they are vigorous in their dramatic force. There are few ballads in the English language more stirring than "The Ballad of East and West," worthy to stand by the Border ballads of Scott.'—*Spectator.*

'The ballads teem with imagination, they palpitate with emotion. We read them with laughter and tears; the metres throb in our pulses, the cunningly ordered words tingle with life; and if this be not poetry, what is?'—*Pall Mall Gazette.*

Henley. LYRA HEROICA: An Anthology selected from the best English Verse of the 16th, 17th, 18th, and 19th Centuries. By WILLIAM ERNEST HENLEY, Author of ' A Book of Verse,' 'Views and Reviews,' etc. *Crown 8vo. Stamped gilt buckram, gilt top, edges uncut. 6s.*

'Mr. Henley has brought to the task of selection an instinct alike for poetry and for chivalry which seems to us quite wonderfully, and even unerringly, right.'—*Guardian.*

Tomson. A SUMMER NIGHT, AND OTHER POEMS. By GRAHAM R. TOMSON. With Frontispiece by A. TOMSON. *Fcap. 8vo. 3s. 6d.*

An edition on hand-made paper, limited to 50 copies. *10s. 6d. net.*

'Mrs. Tomson holds perhaps the very highest rank among poetesses of English birth. This selection will help her reputation.'—*Black and White.*

Ibsen. BRAND. A Drama by HENRIK IBSEN. Translated by WILLIAM WILSON. *Crown 8vo. Second Edition.* 3s. 6d.

'The greatest world-poem of the nineteenth century next to "Faust." "Brand" will have an astonishing interest for Englishmen. It is in the same set with "Agamemnon," with "Lear," with the literature that we now instinctively regard as high and holy.'—*Daily Chronicle.*

"Q." GREEN BAYS : Verses and Parodies. By "Q.," Author of 'Dead Man's Rock' etc. *Second Edition. Fcap. 8vo.* 3s. 6d.

'The verses display a rare and versatile gift of parody, great command of metre, and a very pretty turn of humour.'—*Times.*

"A. G." VERSES TO ORDER. By "A. G." *Cr. 8vo.* 2s. 6d. *net.*

A small volume of verse by a writer whose initials are well known to Oxford men.
'A capital specimen of light academic poetry. These verses are very bright and engaging, easy and sufficiently witty.'—*St. James's Gazette.*

Hosken. VERSES BY THE WAY. By J. D. HOSKEN. *Crown 8vo.* 5s.

A small edition on hand-made paper. *Price* 12s. 6d. *net.*

A Volume of Lyrics and Sonnets by J. D. Hosken, the Postman Poet. Q, the Author of 'The Splendid Spur,' writes a critical and biographical introduction.

Gale. CRICKET SONGS. By NORMAN GALE. *Crown 8vo. Linen.* 2s. 6d.

Also a limited edition on hand-made paper. *Demy 8vo.* 10s. 6d. *net.*

'They are wrung out of the excitement of the moment, and palpitate with the spirit of the game.'—*Star.*
'As healthy as they are spirited, and ought to have a great success.'—*Times.*
'Simple, manly, and humorous. Every cricketer should buy the book.'—*Westminster Gazette.*
'Cricket has never known such a singer.'—*Cricket.*

Langbridge. BALLADS OF THE BRAVE : Poems of Chivalry, Enterprise, Courage, and Constancy, from the Earliest Times to the Present Day. Edited, with Notes, by Rev. F. LANGBRIDGE. *Crown 8vo. Buckram* 3s. 6d. School Edition, 2s. 6d.

'A very happy conception happily carried out. These "Ballads of the Brave" are intended to suit the real tastes of boys, and will suit the taste of the great majority. —*Spectator.*   'The book is full of splendid things.'—*World.*

General Literature

Collingwood. JOHN RUSKIN: His Life and Work. By
W. G. COLLINGWOOD, M.A., late Scholar of University College,
Oxford, Author of the 'Art Teaching of John Ruskin,' Editor of
Mr. Ruskin's Poems. 2 *vols.* *8vo.* 32*s.* *Second Edition.*

This important work is written by Mr. Collingwood, who has been for some years
Mr. Ruskin's private secretary, and who has had unique advantages in obtaining
materials for this book from Mr. Ruskin himself and from his friends. It contains
a large amount of new matter, and of letters which have never been published,
and is, in fact, a full and authoritative biography of Mr. Ruskin. The book
contains numerous portraits of Mr. Ruskin, including a coloured one from a
water-colour portrait by himself, and also 13 sketches, never before published, by
Mr. Ruskin and Mr. Arthur Severn. A bibliography is added.

'No more magnificent volumes have been published for a long time. . . .'—*Times.*

'This most lovingly written and most profoundly interesting book.'—*Daily News.*

'It is long since we have had a biography with such varied delights of substance
and of form. Such a book is a pleasure for the day, and a joy for ever.'—*Daily
Chronicle.*

'Mr. Ruskin could not well have been more fortunate in his biographer.'—*Globe.*

'A noble monument of a noble subject. One of the most beautiful books about one
of the noblest lives of our century.'—*Glasgow Herald.*

Gladstone. THE SPEECHES AND PUBLIC ADDRESSES
OF THE RT. HON. W. E. GLADSTONE, M.P. With Notes
and Introductions. Edited by A. W. HUTTON, M.A. (Librarian of
the Gladstone Library), and H. J. COHEN, M.A. With Portraits.
8vo. *Vols. IX. and X.* 12*s.* 6*d. each.*

Clark Russell. THE LIFE OF ADMIRAL LORD COL-
LINGWOOD. By W. CLARK RUSSELL, Author of 'The Wreck
of the Grosvenor.' With Illustrations by F. BRANGWYN. *Second
Edition. Crown 8vo.* 6*s.*

'A really good book.'—*Saturday Review.*

'A most excellent and wholesome book, which we should like to see in the hands of
every boy in the country.'—*St. James's Gazette.*

Clark. THE COLLEGES OF OXFORD: Their History and
their Traditions. By Members of the University. Edited by A.
CLARK, M.A., Fellow and Tutor of Lincoln College. *8vo.* 12*s.* 6*d.*

'Whether the reader approaches the book as a patriotic member of a college, as an
antiquary, or as a student of the organic growth of college foundation, it will amply
reward his attention.'—*Times.*

'A delightful book, learned and lively.'—*Academy.*

'A work which will certainly be appealed to for many years as the standard book on
the Colleges of Oxford.'—*Athenæum.*

Wells. OXFORD AND OXFORD LIFE. By Members of
the University.   Edited by J. WELLS, M.A., Fellow and Tutor of
Wadham College.   *Crown 8vo.*   *3s. 6d.*

This work contains an account of life at Oxford—intellectual, social, and religious—
a careful estimate of necessary expenses, a review of recent changes, a statement
of the present position of the University, and chapters on Women's Education,
aids to study, and University Extension.

'We congratulate Mr. Wells on the production of a readable and intelligent account
of Oxford as it is at the present time, written by persons who are, with hardly an
exception, possessed of a close acquaintance with the system and life of the
University.'—*Athenæum.*

Perrens. THE HISTORY OF FLORENCE FROM THE
TIME OF THE MEDICIS TO THE FALL OF THE
REPUBLIC.   By F. T. PERRENS.   Translated by HANNAH
LYNCH.   *In Three Volumes.*   *Vol. I.*   *8vo.*   *12s. 6d.*

This is a translation from the French of the best history of Florence in existence.
This volume covers a period of profound interest—political and literary—and
is written with great vivacity.

'This is a standard book by an honest and intelligent historian, who has deserved
well of his countrymen, and of all who are interested in Italian history.'—*Manchester Guardian.*

Browning. GUELPHS AND GHIBELLINES: A Short History
of Mediæval Italy, A.D. 1250-1409.   By OSCAR BROWNING, Fellow
and Tutor of King's College, Cambridge.   *Second Edition.*   *Crown
8vo.*   *5s.*

'A very able book.'—*Westminster Gazette.*

'A vivid picture of mediæval Italy.'—*Standard.*

O'Grady.   THE STORY OF IRELAND.   By STANDISH
O'GRADY, Author of 'Finn and his Companions.'   *Cr. 8vo.*   *2s. 6d.*

'Novel and very fascinating history. Wonderfully alluring.'—*Cork Examiner.*

'Most delightful, most stimulating. Its racy humour, its original imaginings, its
perfectly unique history, make it one of the freshest, breeziest volumes.'—
Methodist Times.

'A survey at once graphic, acute, and quaintly written.'—*Times.*

Dixon. ENGLISH POETRY FROM BLAKE TO BROWN-
ING.   By W. M. DIXON, M.A.   *Crown 8vo.*   *3s. 6d.*

A Popular Account of the Poetry of the Century.

'Scholarly in conception, and full of sound and suggestive criticism.'—*Times.*

'The book is remarkable for freshness of thought expressed in graceful language.'—
Manchester Examiner.

Bowden. THE EXAMPLE OF BUDDHA: Being Quota-
tions from Buddhist Literature for each Day in the Year. Compiled
by E. M. BOWDEN.   With Preface by Sir EDWIN ARNOLD.   *Third
Edition.*   *16mo.*   *2s. 6d.*

Flinders Petrie. TELL EL AMARNA. By W. M. FLINDERS PETRIE, D.C.L. With chapters by Professor A. H. SAYCE, D.D.; F. LL. GRIFFITH, F.S.A.; and F. C. J. SPURRELL, F.G.S. With numerous coloured illustrations. *Royal 4to.* 20s. *net.*

Massee. A MONOGRAPH OF THE MYXOGASTRES. By GEORGE MASSEE. With 12 Coloured Plates. *Royal 8vo.* 18s. *net.*

'A work much in advance of any book in the language treating of this group of organisms. It is indispensable to every student of the Mxyogastres. The coloured plates deserve high praise for their accuracy and execution.'—*Nature.*

Bushill. PROFIT SHARING AND THE LABOUR QUESTION. By T. W. BUSHILL, a Profit Sharing Employer. With an Introduction by SEDLEY TAYLOR, Author of 'Profit Sharing between Capital and Labour.' *Crown 8vo.* 2s. 6d.

John Beever. PRACTICAL FLY-FISHING, Founded on Nature, by JOHN BEEVER, late of the Thwaite House, Coniston. A New Edition, with a Memoir of the Author by W. G. COLLINGWOOD, M.A. Also additional Notes and a chapter on Char-Fishing, by A. and A. R. SEVERN. With a specially designed title-page. *Crown 8vo.* 3s. 6d.

A little book on Fly-Fishing by an old friend of Mr. Ruskin. It has been out of print for some time, and being still much in request, is now issued with a Memoir of the Author by W. G. Collingwood.

Theology

Driver. SERMONS ON SUBJECTS CONNECTED WITH THE OLD TESTAMENT. By S. R. DRIVER, D.D., Canon of Christ Church, Regius Professor of Hebrew in the University of Oxford. *Crown 8vo.* 6s.

'A welcome companion to the author's famous 'Introduction.' No man can read these discourses without feeling that Dr. Driver is fully alive to the deeper teaching of the Old Testament.'—*Guardian.*

Cheyne. FOUNDERS OF OLD TESTAMENT CRITICISM: Biographical, Descriptive, and Critical Studies. By T. K. CHEYNE, D.D., Oriel Professor of the Interpretation of Holy Scripture at Oxford. *Large crown 8vo.* 7s. 6d.

This important book is a historical sketch of O.T. Criticism in the form of biographical studies from the days of Eichhorn to those of Driver and Robertson Smith. It is the only book of its kind in English.

'The volume is one of great interest and value. It displays all the author's well-known ability and learning, and its opportune publication has laid all students of theology, and specially of Bible criticism, under weighty obligation.'—*Scotsman.* A very learned and instructive work.'—*Times.*

Prior. CAMBRIDGE SERMONS. Edited by C. H. PRIOR, M.A., Fellow and Tutor of Pembroke College. *Crown 8vo.* 6s.

A volume of sermons preached before the University of Cambridge by various preachers, including the Archbishop of Canterbury and Bishop Westcott.

'A representative collection. Bishop Westcott's is a noble sermon.'—*Guardian.*

'Full of thoughtfulness and dignity.'—*Record.*

Beeching. BRADFIELD SERMONS. Sermons by H. C. BEECHING, M.A., Rector of Yattendon, Berks. With a Preface by CANON SCOTT HOLLAND. *Crown 8vo.* 2s. 6d.

Seven sermons preached before the boys of Bradfield College.

James. CURIOSITIES OF CHRISTIAN HISTORY PRIOR TO THE REFORMATION. By CROAKE JAMES, Author of 'Curiosities of Law and Lawyers.' *Crown 8vo.* 7s. 6d.

'This volume contains a great deal of quaint and curious matter, affording some "particulars of the interesting persons, episodes, and events from the Christian's point of view during the first fourteen centuries." Wherever we dip into his pages we find something worth dipping into.'—*John Bull.*

Kaufmann. CHARLES KINGSLEY. By M. KAUFMANN, M.A. *Crown 8vo. Buckram.* 5s.

A biography of Kingsley, especially dealing with his achievements in social reform.

'The author has certainly gone about his work with conscientiousness and industry.'— *Sheffield Daily Telegraph.*

Leaders of Religion

Edited by H. C. BEECHING, M.A. *With Portraits, crown 8vo.*

A series of short biographies of the most prominent leaders of religious life and thought of all ages and countries.

2/6 & 3/6

The following are ready—   **2s. 6d.**

CARDINAL NEWMAN. By R. H. HUTTON. *Second Edition.*

'Few who read this book will fail to be struck by the wonderful insight it displays into the nature of the Cardinal's genius and the spirit of his life.'—WILFRID WARD, in the *Tablet.*

'Full of knowledge, excellent in method, and intelligent in criticism. We regard i as wholly admirable.'—*Academy.*

JOHN WESLEY. By J. H. OVERTON, M.A.

'It is well done : the story is clearly told, proportion is duly observed, and there is no lack either of discrimination or of sympathy.'—*Manchester Guardian.*

BISHOP WILBERFORCE. By G. W. DANIEL, M.A.
CARDINAL MANNING. By A. W. HUTTON, M.A.
CHARLES SIMEON. By H. C. G. MOULE, M.A.

3s. 6d.

JOHN KEBLE. By WALTER LOCK, M.A. *Seventh Edition.*
THOMAS CHALMERS. By Mrs. OLIPHANT. *Second Edition.*
Other volumes will be announced in due course.

Works by S. Baring Gould

OLD COUNTRY LIFE. With Sixty-seven Illustrations by
W. PARKINSON, F. D. BEDFORD, and F. MASEY. *Large Crown
8vo, cloth super extra, top edge gilt,* 10s. 6d. *Fourth and Cheaper
Edition.* 6s.

'"Old Country Life," as healthy wholesome reading, full of breezy life and movement, full of quaint stories vigorously told, will not be excelled by any book to be
published throughout the year. Sound, hearty, and English to the core.'—*World.*

HISTORIC ODDITIES AND STRANGE EVENTS. *Third
Edition. Crown 8vo.* 6s.

'A collection of exciting and entertaining chapters. The whole volume is delightful
reading.'—*Times.*

FREAKS OF FANATICISM. *Third Edition. Crown 8vo.* 6s.

'Mr. Baring Gould has a keen eye for colour and effect, and the subjects he has
chosen give ample scope to his descriptive and analytic faculties. A perfectly
fascinating book.'—*Scottish Leader.*

SONGS OF THE WEST: Traditional Ballads and Songs of
the West of England, with their Traditional Melodies. Collected
by S. BARING GOULD, M.A., and H. FLEETWOOD SHEPPARD,
M.A. Arranged for Voice and Piano. In 4 Parts (containing 25
Songs each), *Parts I., II., III.,* 3s. *each. Part IV.,* 5s. *In one
Vol., French morocco,* 15s.

'A rich and varied collection of humour, pathos, grace, and poetic fancy.'—*Saturday
Review.*

YORKSHIRE ODDITIES AND STRANGE EVENTS.
Fourth Edition. Crown 8vo. 6s.

STRANGE SURVIVALS AND SUPERSTITIONS. With

Illustrations. By S. BARING GOULD. *Crown 8vo. Second Edition.*
6s.

A book on such subjects as Foundations, Gables, Holes, Gallows, Raising the Hat, Old
Ballads, etc. etc. It traces in a most interesting manner their origin and history.
'We have read Mr. Baring Gould's book from beginning to end. It is full of quaint
and various information, and there is not a dull page in it.'—*Notes and Queries.*

THE TRAGEDY OF THE CAESARS: The

Emperors of the Julian and Claudian Lines. With numerous Illus
trations from Busts, Gems, Cameos, etc. By S. BARING GOULD,
Author of 'Mehalah,' etc. *Third Edition. Royal 8vo.* 15s.

'A most splendid and fascinating book on a subject of undying interest. The great
feature of the book is the use the author has made of the existing portraits of the
Caesars, and the admirable critical subtlety he has exhibited in dealing with this
line of research. It is brilliantly written, and the illustrations are supplied on a
scale of profuse magnificence.'—*Daily Chronicle.*
'The volumes will in no sense disappoint the general reader. Indeed, in their way,
there is nothing in any sense so good in English. . . . Mr. Baring Gould has
presented his narrative in such a way as not to make one dull page.'—*Athenæum.*

MR. BARING GOULD'S NOVELS

'To say that a book is by the author of "Mehalah" is to imply that it contains a
story cast on strong lines, containing dramatic possibilities, vivid and sympathetic
descriptions of Nature, and a wealth of ingenious imagery.'—*Speaker.*
'That whatever Mr. Baring Gould writes is well worth reading, is a conclusion that
may be very generally accepted. His views of life are fresh and vigorous, his
language pointed and characteristic, the incidents of which he makes use are
striking and original, his characters are life-like, and though somewhat exceptional people, are drawn and coloured with artistic force. Add to this that his
descriptions of scenes and scenery are painted with the loving eyes and skilled
hands of a master of his art, that he is always fresh and never dull, and under
such conditions it is no wonder that readers have gained confidence both in his
power of amusing and satisfying them, and that year by year his popularity
widens.'—*Court Circular.*

SIX SHILLINGS EACH

IN THE ROAR OF THE SEA : A Tale of the Cornish Coast.
MRS. CURGENVEN OF CURGENVEN.
CHEAP JACK ZITA.
THE QUEEN OF LOVE.

THREE SHILLINGS AND SIXPENCE EACH

ARMINELL : A Social Romance.
URITH : A Story of Dartmoor.
MARGERY OF QUETHER, and other Stories.
JACQUETTA, and other Stories.

Fiction

SIX SHILLING NOVELS

Corelli. BARABBAS : A DREAM OF THE WORLD'S TRAGEDY. By MARIE CORELLI, Author of 'A Romance of Two Worlds,' 'Vendetta,' etc. *Eleventh Edition. Crown 8vo. 6s.*

Miss Corelli's new romance has been received with much disapprobation by the secular papers, and with warm welcome by the religious papers. By the former she has been accused of blasphemy and bad taste; 'a gory nightmare'; 'a hideous travesty'; 'grotesque vulgarisation'; 'unworthy of criticism'; 'vulgar redundancy'; 'sickening details'—these are some of the secular flowers of speech. On the other hand, the 'Guardian' praises 'the dignity of its conceptions, the reserve round the Central Figure, the fine imagery of the scene and circumstance, so much that is elevating and devout'; the 'Illustrated Church News' styles the book 'reverent and artistic, broad based on the rock of our common nature, and appealing to what is best in it'; the 'Christian World' says it is written 'by one who has more than conventional reverence, who has tried to tell the story that it may be read again with open and attentive eyes'; the 'Church of England Pulpit' welcomes 'a book which teems with faith without any appearance of irreverence.'

Benson. DODO: A DETAIL OF THE DAY. By E. F. BENSON. *Crown 8vo. Fourteenth Edition. 6s.*

A story of society by a new writer, full of interest and power, which has attracted by its brilliance universal attention. The best critics were cordial in their praise. The 'Guardian' spoke of 'Dodo' as *unusually clever and interesting*; the 'Spectator' called it *a delightfully witty sketch of society*; the 'Speaker' said the dialogue was *a perpetual feast of epigram and paradox*; the 'Athenæum' spoke of the author as *a writer of quite exceptional ability*; the 'Academy' praised his *amazing cleverness*; the 'World' said the book was *brilliantly written*; and half-a-dozen papers declared there was *not a dull page in the book.*

Baring Gould. IN THE ROAR OF THE SEA : A Tale of the Cornish Coast. By S. BARING GOULD. *New Edition. 6s.*

Baring Gould. MRS. CURGENVEN OF CURGENVEN. By S. BARING GOULD. *Third Edition. 6s.*

A story of Devon life. The 'Graphic' speaks of it as *a novel of vigorous humour and sustained power*; the 'Sussex Daily News' says that *the swing of the narrative is splendid*; and the 'Speaker' mentions its *bright imaginative power.*

Baring Gould. CHEAP JACK ZITA. By S. BARING GOULD. *Third Edition. Crown 8vo. 6s.*

A Romance of the Ely Fen District in 1815, which the 'Westminster Gazette' calls 'a powerful drama of human passion'; and the 'National Observer' 'a story worthy the author.'

Baring Gould. THE QUEEN OF LOVE. By S. BARING GOULD. *Second Edition. Crown 8vo. 6s.*

The 'Glasgow Herald' says that 'the scenery is admirable, and the dramatic incidents are most striking.' The 'Westminster Gazette' calls the book 'strong, interesting, and clever.' 'Punch' says that 'you cannot put it down until you have finished it.' 'The Sussex Daily News' says that it 'can be heartily recommended to all who care for cleanly, energetic, and interesting fiction.'

Norris. HIS GRACE. By W. E. NORRIS, Author of ' Mademoiselle de Mersac.' *Third Edition. Crown 8vo.* 6s.

'The characters are delineated by the author with his characteristic skill and vivacity, and the story is told with that ease of manners and Thackerayean insight which give strength of flavour to Mr. Norris's novels No one can depict the Englishwoman of the better classes with more subtlety.'—*Glasgow Herald.*

' Mr. Norris has drawn a really fine character in the Duke of Hurstbourne, at once unconventional and very true to the conventionalities of life, weak and strong in a breath, capable of inane follies and heroic decisions, yet not so definitely portrayed as to relieve a reader of the necessity of study on his own behalf.'—*Athenæum.*

Parker. MRS. FALCHION. By GILBERT PARKER, Author of ' Pierre and His People.' *New Edition.* 6s.

Mr. Parker's second book has received a warm welcome. The ' Athenæum' called it *a splendid study of character*; the ' Pall Mall Gazette' spoke of the writing as *but little behind anything that has been done by any writer of our time*; the ' St. James's' called it *a very striking and admirable novel*; and the ' Westminster Gazette' applied to it the epithet of *distinguished.*

Parker. PIERRE AND HIS PEOPLE. By GILBERT PARKER. *Crown 8vo. Buckram.* 6s.

'Stories happily conceived and finely executed. There is strength and genius in Mr. Parker's style.'—*Daily Telegraph.*

Parker. THE TRANSLATION OF A SAVAGE. By GILBERT PARKER, Author of ' Pierre and His People,' ' Mrs. Falchion,' etc. *Crown 8vo.* 5s.

'The plot is original and one difficult to work out; but Mr. Parker has done it with great skill and delicacy. The reader who is not interested in this original, fresh, and well-told tale must be a dull person indeed.'—*Daily Chronicle.*

'A strong and successful piece of workmanship. The portrait of Lali, strong, dignified, and pure, is exceptionally well drawn.'—*Manchester Guardian.*

'A very pretty and interesting story, and Mr. Parker tells it with much skill. The story is one to be read.'—*St. James's Gazette.*

Anthony Hope. A CHANGE OF AIR: A Novel. By ANTHONY HOPE, Author of ' The Prisoner of Zenda,' etc. *Crown 8vo.* 6s.

A bright story by Mr. Hope, who has, the *Athenæum* says, 'a decided outlook and individuality of his own.'

' A graceful, vivacious comedy, true to human nature. The characters are traced with a masterly hand.'—*Times.*

Pryce. TIME AND THE WOMAN. By RICHARD PRYCE, Author of ' Miss Maxwell's Affections,' ' The Quiet Mrs. Fleming,' etc. New and Cheaper Edition. *Crown 8vo.* 6s.

' Mr. Pryce's work recalls the style of Octave Feuillet, by its clearness, conciseness, its literary reserve.'—*Athenæum.*

Marriott Watson. DIOGENES OF LONDON and other Sketches. By H. B. MARRIOTT WATSON, Author of 'The Web of the Spider.' *Crown 8vo. Buckram. 6s.*

'By all those who delight in the uses of words, who rate the exercise of prose above the exercise of verse, who rejoice in all proofs of its delicacy and its strength, who believe that English prose is chief among the moulds of thought, by these Mr. Marriott Watson's book will be welcomed.'—*National Observer.*

Gilchrist. THE STONE DRAGON. By MURRAY GILCHRIST. *Crown 8vo. Buckram. 6s.*

'The author's faults are atoned for by certain positive and admirable merits. The romances have not their counterpart in modern literature, and to read them is a unique experience.'—*National Observer.*

THREE-AND-SIXPENNY NOVELS

Baring Gould. ARMINELL: A Social Romance. By S. BARING GOULD. *New Edition. Crown 8vo. 3s. 6d.*

Baring Gould. URITH: A Story of Dartmoor. By S. BARING GOULD. *Third Edition. Crown 8vo. 3s. 6d.*
'The author is at his best.'—*Times.*
'He has nearly reached the high water-mark of " Mehalah." '—*National Observer.*

Baring Gould. MARGERY OF QUETHER, and other Stories. By S. BARING GOULD. *Crown 8vo. 3s. 6d.*

Baring Gould. JACQUETTA, and other Stories. By S. BARING GOULD. *Crown 8vo. 3s. 6d.*

Gray. ELSA. A Novel. By E. M'QUEEN GRAY. *Crown 8vo. 3s. 6d.*
'A charming novel. The characters are not only powerful sketches, but minutely and carefully finished portraits.'—*Guardian.*

Pearce. JACO TRELOAR. By J. H. PEARCE, Author of 'Esther Pentreath.' *New Edition. Crown 8vo. 3s. 6d.*
A tragic story of Cornish life by a writer of remarkable power, whose first novel has been highly praised by Mr. Gladstone.
The 'Spectator' speaks of Mr. Pearce as *a writer of exceptional power*; the 'Daily Telegraph' calls the book *powerful and picturesque*; the 'Birmingham Post' asserts that it is *a novel of high quality.*

Edna Lyall. DERRICK VAUGHAN, NOVELIST. By EDNA LYALL, Author of 'Donovan,' etc. *Crown 8vo. 3s. 6d.*

Clark Russell. MY DANISH SWEETHEART. By W. CLARK RUSSELL, Author of 'The Wreck of the Grosvenor,' etc. *Illustrated. Third Edition. Crown 8vo. 3s. 6d.*

Author of 'Vera.' THE DANCE OF THE HOURS. By the Author of 'Vera.' *Crown 8vo.* 3s. 6d.

Esmè Stuart. A WOMAN OF FORTY. By ESMÈ STUART, Author of 'Muriel's Marriage,' 'Virginie's Husband,' etc. *New Edition. Crown 8vo.* 3s. 6d.
'The story is well written, and some of the scenes show great dramatic power. — *Daily Chronicle.*

Fenn. THE STAR GAZERS. By G. MANVILLE FENN, Author of 'Eli's Children,' etc. *New Edition. Cr. 8vo.* 3s. 6d.
'A stirring romance.'—*Western Morning News.*
'Told with all the dramatic power for which Mr. Fenn is conspicuous.'—*Bradford Observer.*

Dickinson. A VICAR'S WIFE. By EVELYN DICKINSON. *Crown 8vo.* 3s. 6d.

Prowse. THE POISON OF ASPS. By R. ORTON PROWSE. *Crown 8vo.* 3s. 6d.

Grey. THE STORY OF CHRIS. By ROWLAND GREY. *Crown 8vo.* 5s.

Lynn Linton. THE TRUE HISTORY OF JOSHUA DAVIDSON, Christian and Communist. By E. LYNN LINTON. Eleventh Edition. *Post 8vo.* 1s.

HALF-CROWN NOVELS

A Series of Novels by popular Authors, tastefully bound in cloth. **2/6**

1. THE PLAN OF CAMPAIGN. By F. MABEL ROBINSON.
2. DISENCHANTMENT. By F. MABEL ROBINSON.
3. MR. BUTLER'S WARD. By F. MABEL ROBINSON.
4. HOVENDEN, V.C. By F. MABEL ROBINSON.
5. ELI'S CHILDREN. By G. MANVILLE FENN.
6. A DOUBLE KNOT. By G. MANVILLE FENN.
7. DISARMED. By M. BETHAM EDWARDS.
8. A LOST ILLUSION. By LESLIE KEITH.
9. A MARRIAGE AT SEA. By W. CLARK RUSSELL.

10. IN TENT AND BUNGALOW. By the Author of 'Indian Idylls.'

11. MY STEWARDSHIP. By E. M'QUEEN GRAY.

12. A REVEREND GENTLEMAN. By J. M. COBBAN.

13. A DEPLORABLE AFFAIR. By W. E. NORRIS.

14. JACK'S FATHER. By W. E. NORRIS.

Other volumes will be announced in due course.

Books for Boys and Girls

Baring Gould. THE ICELANDER'S SWORD. By S. BARING GOULD, Author of 'Mehalah,' etc. With Twenty-nine Illustrations by J. MOYR SMITH. *Crown 8vo. 6s.*

A stirring story of Iceland, written for boys by the author of ' In the Roar of the Sea.

Cuthell. TWO LITTLE CHILDREN AND CHING. By EDITH E. CUTHELL. Profusely Illustrated. *Crown 8vo. Cloth, gilt edges. 3s. 6d.*

Another story, with a dog hero, by the author of the very popular ' Only a Guard-Room Dog.'

Blake. TODDLEBEN'S HERO. By M. M. BLAKE, Author of 'The Siege of Norwich Castle.' With 36 Illustrations. *Crown 8vo. 3s. 6d.*

A story of military life for children.

Cuthell. ONLY A GUARD-ROOM DOG. By Mrs. CUTHELL. With 16 Illustrations by W. PARKINSON. *Square Crown 8vo. 3s. 6d.*

'This is a charming story. Tangle was but a little mongrel Skye terrier, but he had a big heart in his little body, and played a hero's part more than once. The book can be warmly recommended.'—*Standard.*

Collingwood. THE DOCTOR OF THE JULIET. By HARRY COLLINGWOOD, Author of 'The Pirate Island,' etc. Illustrated by GORDON BROWNE. *Crown 8vo. 3s. 6d.*

'"The Doctor of the Juliet," well illustrated by Gordon Browne, is one of Harry Collingwood's best efforts.'—*Morning Post.*

Clark Russell. MASTER ROCKAFELLAR'S VOYAGE. By
W. CLARK RUSSELL, Author of 'The Wreck of the Grosvenor,' etc.
Illustrated by GORDON BROWNE. *Second Edition.* *Crown 8vo.*
3s. 6d.

'Mr. Clark Russell's story of "Master Rockafellar's Voyage" will be among the
favourites of the Christmas books. There is a rattle and "go" all through it, and
its illustrations are charming in themselves, and very much above the average in
the way in which they are produced.'—*Guardian.*

Manville Fenn. SYD BELTON : Or, The Boy who would not
go to Sea. By G. MANVILLE FENN, Author of 'In the King's
Name,' etc. Illustrated by GORDON BROWNE. *Crown 8vo.* 3s. 6d.

Who among the young story-reading public will not rejoice at the sight of the old
combination, so often proved admirable—a story by Manville Fenn, illustrated
by Gordon Browne? The story, too, is one of the good old sort, full of life and
vigour, breeziness and fun.'—*Journal of Education.*

The Peacock Library

A Series of Books for Girls by well-known Authors,
handsomely bound in blue and silver, and well illustrated. **3/6**
Crown 8vo.

1. A PINCH OF EXPERIENCE. By L. B. WALFORD.
2. THE RED GRANGE. By Mrs. MOLESWORTH.
3. THE SECRET OF MADAME DE MONLUC. By the
   Author of ' Mdle Mori.'
4. DUMPS. By Mrs. PARR, Author of 'Adam and Eve.'
5. OUT OF THE FASHION. By L. T. MEADE.
6. A GIRL OF THE PEOPLE. By L. T. MEADE.
7. HEPSY GIPSY. By L. T. MEADE. 2s. 6d.
8. THE HONOURABLE MISS. By L. T. MEADE.
9. MY LAND OF BEULAH. By Mrs. LEITH ADAMS.

University Extension Series

A series of books on historical, literary, and scientific subjects, suitable
for extension students and home reading circles. Each volume is com-

plete in itself, and the subjects are treated by competent writers in a broad and philosophic spirit.

Edited by J. E. SYMES, M.A.,

Principal of University College, Nottingham.

Crown 8vo. Price (with some exceptions) 2s. 6d.

The following volumes are ready :—

THE INDUSTRIAL HISTORY OF ENGLAND. By H. DE B. GIBBINS, M.A., late Scholar of Wadham College, Oxon., Cobden Prizeman. *Third Edition.* With Maps and Plans. 3*s.*

'A compact and clear story of our industrial development. A study of this concise but luminous book cannot fail to give the reader a clear insight into the principal phenomena of our industrial history. The editor and publishers are to be congratulated on this first volume of their venture, and we shall look with expectant interest for the succeeding volumes of the series.'—*University Extension Journal.*

A HISTORY OF ENGLISH POLITICAL ECONOMY. By L. L. PRICE, M.A., Fellow of Oriel College, Oxon.

PROBLEMS OF POVERTY: An Inquiry into the Industrial Conditions of the Poor. By J. A. HOBSON, M.A.

VICTORIAN POETS. By A. SHARP.

THE FRENCH REVOLUTION. By J. E. SYMES, M.A.

PSYCHOLOGY. By F. S. GRANGER, M.A., Lecturer in Philosophy at University College, Nottingham.

THE EVOLUTION OF PLANT LIFE: Lower Forms. By G. MASSEE, Kew Gardens. With Illustrations.

AIR AND WATER. Professor V. B. LEWES, M.A. Illustrated.

THE CHEMISTRY OF LIFE AND HEALTH. By C. W. KIMMINS, M.A. Camb. Illustrated.

THE MECHANICS OF DAILY LIFE. By V. P. SELLS, M.A. Illustrated.

ENGLISH SOCIAL REFORMERS. H. DE B. GIBBINS, M.A.

ENGLISH TRADE AND FINANCE IN THE SEVEN-TEENTH CENTURY. By W. A. S. HEWINS, B.A.

THE CHEMISTRY OF FIRE. The Elementary Principles of Chemistry. By M. M. PATTISON MUIR, M.A. Illustrated.

A TEXT-BOOK OF AGRICULTURAL BOTANY. By M. C. POTTER, M.A., F.L.S. Illustrated. 3*s. 6d.*

THE VAULT OF HEAVEN. A Popular Introduction to Astronomy. By R. A. GREGORY. With numerous Illustrations.

METEOROLOGY. The Elements of Weather and Climate. By H. N. DICKSON, F.R.S.E., F.R. Met. Soc. Illustrated.

A MANUAL OF ELECTRICAL SCIENCE. By GEORGE J. BURCH, M.A. With numerous Illustrations. 3s.

Social Questions of To-day

Edited by H. DE B. GIBBINS, M.A.

Crown 8vo.   2s. 6d.

2/6

A series of volumes upon those topics of social, economic, and industrial interest that are at the present moment fore-most in the public mind. Each volume of the series is written by an author who is an acknowledged authority upon the subject with which he deals.

The following Volumes of the Series are ready :—

TRADE UNIONISM—NEW AND OLD. By G. HOWELL, M.P., Author of 'The Conflicts of Capital and Labour.' *Second Edition.*

THE CO-OPERATIVE MOVEMENT TO-DAY. By G. J. HOLYOAKE, Author of ' The History of Co-operation.'

MUTUAL THRIFT. By Rev. J. FROME WILKINSON, M.A., Author of ' The Friendly Society Movement.'

PROBLEMS OF POVERTY : An Inquiry into the Industrial Conditions of the Poor. By J. A. HOBSON, M.A.

THE COMMERCE OF NATIONS. By C. F. BASTABLE, M.A., Professor of Economics at Trinity College, Dublin.

THE ALIEN INVASION. By W. H. WILKINS, B.A., Secretary to the Society for Preventing the Immigration of Destitute Aliens.

THE RURAL EXODUS. By P. ANDERSON GRAHAM.

LAND NATIONALIZATION. By HAROLD COX, B.A.

A SHORTER WORKING DAY. By H. DE B. GIBBINS and R. A. HADFIELD, of the Hecla Works, Sheffield.

BACK TO THE LAND : An Inquiry into the Cure for Rural Depopulation. By H. E. MOORE.

TRUSTS, POOLS AND CORNERS: As affecting Commerce and Industry. By J. STEPHEN JEANS, M.R.I., F.S.S.

THE FACTORY SYSTEM. By R. COOKE TAYLOR.

THE STATE AND ITS CHILDREN. By GERTRUDE TUCKWELL.

Classical Translations

Edited by H. F. FOX, M.A., Fellow and Tutor of Brasenose College, Oxford.

Messrs. Methuen propose to issue a New Series of Translations from the Greek and Latin Classics. They have enlisted the services of some of the best Oxford and Cambridge Scholars, and it is their intention that the Series shall be distinguished by literary excellence as well as by scholarly accuracy.

Crown 8vo.   Finely printed and bound in blue buckram.

CICERO—De Oratore I. Translated by E. N. P. MOOR, M.A., Assistant Master at Clifton. 3s. 6d.

ÆSCHYLUS—Agamemnon, Chöephoroe, Eumenides. Translated by LEWIS CAMPBELL, LL.D., late Professor of Greek at St. Andrews. 5s.

LUCIAN—Six Dialogues (Nigrinus, Icaro-Menippus, The Cock, The Ship, The Parasite, The Lover of Falsehood). Translated by S. T. IRWIN, M.A., Assistant Master at Clifton; late Scholar of Exeter College, Oxford. 3s. 6d.

SOPHOCLES—Electra and Ajax. Translated by E. D. A. MORSHEAD, M.A., late Scholar of New College, Oxford; Assistant Master at Winchester. 2s. 6d.

TACITUS—Agricola and Germania. Translated by R. B. TOWNSHEND, late Scholar of Trinity College, Cambridge. 2s. 6d.

CICERO—Select Orations (Pro Milone, Pro Murena, Philippic II., In Catilinam). Translated by H. E. D. BLAKISTON, M.A., Fellow and Tutor of Trinity College, Oxford. 5s.

Methuen's Commercial Series

BRITISH COMMERCE AND COLONIES FROM ELIZABETH TO VICTORIA. By H. DE B. GIBBINS, M.A., Author of 'The Industrial History of England,' etc., etc. 2s.

A MANUAL OF FRENCH COMMERCIAL CORRES-
PONDENCE. By S. E. BALLY, Modern Language Master at
the Manchester Grammar School. 2s.

COMMERCIAL GEOGRAPHY, with special reference to Trade
Routes, New Markets, and Manufacturing Districts. By L. D.
LYDE, M.A., of The Academy, Glasgow. 2s.

COMMERCIAL EXAMINATION PAPERS. By H. DE B.
GIBBINS, M.A. 1s. 6d.

THE ECONOMICS OF COMMERCE. By H. DE B. GIBBINS,
M.A. 1s. 6d.

A PRIMER OF BUSINESS. By S. JACKSON, M.A. 1s. 6d.

COMMERCIAL ARITHMETIC. By F. G. TAYLOR,
M.A. 1s. 6d.

Works by A. M. M. Stedman, M.A.

INITIA LATINA : Easy Lessons on Elementary Accidence.
Second Edition. Fcap. 8vo. 1s.

FIRST LATIN LESSONS. *Fourth Edition Crown 8vo.* 2s.

FIRST LATIN READER. With Notes adapted to the Shorter
Latin Primer and Vocabulary. *Second Edition. Crown 8vo.* 1s. 6d.

EASY SELECTIONS FROM CAESAR. Part I. The Helvetian War. 18mo. 1s.

EASY SELECTIONS FROM LIVY. Part I. The Kings of
Rome. 18mo. 1s. 6d.

EASY LATIN PASSAGES FOR UNSEEN TRANSLATION.
Third Edition. Fcap. 8vo. 1s. 6d.

EXEMPLA LATINA : First Exercises in Latin Accidence.
With Vocabulary. *Crown 8vo.* 1s.

EASY LATIN EXERCISES ON THE SYNTAX OF THE
SHORTER AND REVISED LATIN PRIMER. With Vocabu-
lary. *Fourth Edition. Crown 8vo.* 2s. 6d. Issued with the con-
sent of Dr. Kennedy.

THE LATIN COMPOUND SENTENCE RULES AND
EXERCISES. *Crown 8vo.* 2s. With Vocabulary. 2s. 6d.

NOTANDA QUAEDAM: Miscellaneous Latin Exercises on Common Rules and Idioms. With Vocabulary. *Second Edition.* *Fcap. 8vo.* 1*s.* 6*d.*

LATIN VOCABULARIES FOR REPETITION: Arranged according to Subjects. *Fourth Edition.* *Fcap. 8vo.* 1*s.* 6*d.*

A VOCABULARY OF LATIN IDIOMS AND PHRASES. 18*mo.* 1*s.*

LATIN EXAMINATION PAPERS IN MISCELLANEOUS GRAMMAR AND IDIOMS. *Fourth Edition.*
A KEY, issued to Tutors and Private Students only, to be had on application to the Publishers. *Second Edition. Crown 8vo.* 6s.

STEPS TO GREEK. 18*mo.* 1*s.* 6*d.*

EASY GREEK PASSAGES FOR UNSEEN TRANSLATION. *Fcap. 8vo.* 1*s.* 6*d.*

EASY GREEK EXERCISES ON ELEMENTARY SYNTAX.
[*In preparation.*

GREEK VOCABULARIES FOR REPETITION: Arranged according to Subjects. *Second Edition. Fcap. 8vo.* 1*s.* 6*d.*

GREEK TESTAMENT SELECTIONS. For the use of Schools. *Third Edition.* With Introduction, Notes, and Vocabulary. *Fcap. 8vo.* 2*s.* 6*d.*

GREEK EXAMINATION PAPERS IN MISCELLANEOUS GRAMMAR AND IDIOMS. *Third Edition.* KEY (issued as above). 6*s.*

STEPS TO FRENCH. 18*mo.* 8*d.*

FIRST FRENCH LESSONS. *Crown 8vo.* 1*s.*

EASY FRENCH PASSAGES FOR UNSEEN TRANSLATION. *Second Edition. Fcap. 8vo.* 1*s.* 6*d.*

EASY FRENCH EXERCISES ON ELEMENTARY SYNTAX. With Vocabulary. *Crown 8vo.* 2*s.* 6*d.*

FRENCH VOCABULARIES FOR REPETITION: Arranged according to Subjects. *Third Edition. Fcap. 8vo.* 1*s.*

FRENCH EXAMINATION PAPERS IN MISCELLANEOUS GRAMMAR AND IDIOMS. *Seventh Edition. Crown 8vo.* 2*s.* 6*d.* KEY (issued as above). 6*s.*

GENERAL KNOWLEDGE EXAMINATION PAPERS. *Second Edition. Crown 8vo.* 2*s.* 6*d.* KEY (issued as above). 7*s.*

School Examination Series

Edited by A. M. M. STEDMAN, M.A.   *Crown 8vo.*   2s. 6d.

FRENCH EXAMINATION PAPERS IN MISCELLANE-
OUS GRAMMAR AND IDIOMS. By A. M. M. STEDMAN, M.A.
Sixth Edition.

A KEY, issued to Tutors and Private Students only, to be had on
application to the Publishers. *Second Edition. Crown 8vo.* 6s.

LATIN EXAMINATION PAPERS IN MISCELLANEOUS
GRAMMAR AND IDIOMS. By A. M. M. STEDMAN, M.A.
Fourth Edition. KEY (issued as above). 6s.

GREEK EXAMINATION PAPERS IN MISCELLANEOUS
GRAMMAR AND IDIOMS. By A. M. M. STEDMAN, M.A.
Third Edition. KEY (issued as above). 6s.

GERMAN EXAMINATION PAPERS IN MISCELLANE-
OUS GRAMMAR AND IDIOMS. By R. J. MORICH, Manchester. *Third Edition.* KEY (issued as above). 6s.

HISTORY AND GEOGRAPHY EXAMINATION PAPERS.
By C. H. SPENCE, M.A., Clifton College.

SCIENCE EXAMINATION PAPERS. By R. E. STEEL, M.A.,
F.C.S., Chief Natural Science Master Bradford Grammar School.
In three vols. Part I., Chemistry ; *Part II.,* Physics.

GENERAL KNOWLEDGE EXAMINATION PAPERS.
By A. M. M. STEDMAN, M.A. *Second Edition.* KEY (issued as
above). 7s.

Primary Classics

With Introductions, Notes, and Vocabularies. 18mo.   1s. *and* 1s. 6d.

FIRST LATIN READER. By A. M. M. STEDMAN, M.A. 1s. 6d.

EASY SELECTIONS FROM CAESAR—THE HELVETIAN
WAR. Edited by A. M. M. STEDMAN, M.A. 1s.

EASY SELECTIONS FROM LIVY—THE KINGS OF
ROME. Edited by A. M. M. STEDMAN, M.A. 1s. 6d.

EASY SELECTIONS FROM HERODOTUS—THE PER-
SIAN WARS. Edited by A. G. LIDDELL, M.A. 1s. 6d.